Praise for Le̶̶̶
and her Lucy Stone Mysteries

TRICK OR TREAT MURDER

"Enjoy Halloween with Lucy Stone and a wicked mystery."
—*Mystery Lover's Bookshop News*

". . . an unusual and enjoyable character. A light-hearted read."
—*The Midwest Book Review*

TIPPY TOE MURDER

"A solid mystery." —*San Francisco Chronicle*

"A surprising and intelligently constructed plot."
—*Cape Cod Times*

MAIL ORDER MURDER

"Will leave readers waiting to place a second order." —*Booklist*

"The writing is skillful and the evocation of small-town New England true. First-time author Leslie Meier more than holds her own."
—*Cleveland Plain Dealer*

"Meier writes about Christmas in a small town with sparkle and warmth." —*Chicago Sun Times*

"An enjoyable read." —*L.A. Life*

Don't miss Leslie Meier's newest Lucy Stone mystery,
BACK TO SCHOOL MURDER, now on sale wherever
hardcover mysteries are sold!

A Lucy Stone Mystery

TRICK OR TREAT
MURDER

Leslie Meier

KENSINGTON BOOKS
Kensington Publishing Corp.
http://www.kensingtonbooks.com

For Mommy,
who always wore her real pearls

KENSINGTON BOOKS are published by

Kensington Publishing Corp.
850 Third Avenue
New York, NY 10022

First Kensington Hardcover Printing: October, 1996
First Kensington Paperback Printing: October, 1997
10 9 8 7 6 5 4 3 2 1

Printed in the United States of America

PROLOGUE

"I could just kill him."

Monica Mayes pressed the gas pedal of her little BMW to the floor and zoomed around a pokey Dodge Caravan, cutting it a bit too close as she pulled back into her lane. The driver of the Caravan braked, and the van swerved, but Monica didn't notice.

"How could he do this to me?" she asked herself, pulling out the cigarette lighter. With a trembling hand she held it to the end of a Virginia Slim and took a long, slow draw. No longer used to the smoke, she hadn't had a cigarette in years, she coughed.

"He's not worth it," she decided, tossing the cigarette out the window. She was damned if she was going to sacrifice her health for him. He'd gotten enough from her already. Thirty-two years of marriage, three grown children.

Tears welled in her eyes. She couldn't believe how much it hurt, actual physical pain. Her chest ached with every breath; she could hardly swallow. He'd never laid a finger on her, but she felt bruised and beaten anyway.

She hadn't seen that final blow coming. If she had she might have taken care to avoid it. But she'd never suspected a thing.

She'd left the house at a quarter to one for her weekly shift at the Hospital Auxiliary thrift shop. Realizing she'd forgotten a couple of Roland's old suits that she'd planned to donate, she returned home. She'd hurried upstairs, thrown open the bedroom door, and was halfway across the room before she even saw them.

Roland and Krissy, her aerobics instructor. Her aerobics instructor, for God's sake! And in her own bed—their marriage bed.

"How could he do that?" she asked herself. He was such a bastard. Why hadn't she realized it sooner? She'd just gotten used to it. She gave and he took. That's the way it was. Her job was to please him. She cooked for him. She cleaned for him. She washed and ironed for him. She entertained for him, and decorated the house for him. She dressed for him, and dieted, and even took aerobics for him.

She'd been a fool. She'd thought their marriage was as important to him as it was to her. Him. The doctor. The head honcho. The chief of staff.

Angry now, she impatiently brushed the tears from her cheeks. She'd show him, she decided. She'd hit him where it hurt. He wasn't going to get off scot free. He'd have to pay. She began making a mental list as she flew along the turnpike, empty on this weekday night now that the tourist season was over.

First of all, she wanted the house in Tinker's Cove, and all the furniture. She'd need her car, of course, and money. A nice little next egg, plus a big fat alimony check every month. It was her due. She'd earned it. She wasn't going to settle for less.

Was that her exit already? Braking hard she careened off the highway, almost losing control of the car on the tight curve of the exit ramp. Shaken, she pulled to a stop at the intersection and paused, taking a few deep breaths. Then she proceeded, carefully turning onto Route One and was soon driving down Main Street, surprised to find it empty. Of course, she reminded herself. Until now, she had only been here in the summer, when the town was full of tourists and summer residents. Now it was fall. Dark came much earlier, and the only signs of life were the lighted windows of the houses.

She stopped at the blinker and turned left, then left again onto Hopkins Homestead Road. The road was named for her house. Hopkins Homestead, the oldest house in Tinker's Cove.

She took one last turn onto the familiar dirt driveway and parked the car neatly in the vine covered carport behind the woodshed.

Her key turned easily in the lock and the heavy pine door swung open. She eagerly inhaled the spicy, old wood smell of the house.

Ignoring her reflection in the spotted glass of the hall mirror she stepped into the tiny parlor and switched on a lamp.

It was just as she remembered. Bare, wide plank floors, a camelback sofa, a scarred old sea chest serving as a coffee table. There were no curtains on the windows; Monica loved the way the garden became an Impressionist landscape when viewed through the wavy old glass. Anyone passing the house could have looked in and seen her, but no one did.

She went into the next room, the dining room. A collection of Currier and Ives lithographs hung on the wall, and a pine drop leaf table stood in the center of the room, surrounded by six yellow painted chairs. The chairs were the first purchase she'd made for the old house, hesitantly raising her hand at a country auction.

"Sold," announced the auctioneer, bringing down his gavel. The bidding was over almost before it had begun. Soon she'd become a regular, rescuing fine antiques from the greedy dealers who stripped off the original finishes and slapped on high prices, taking advantage of ignorant buyers.

Passing through the kitchen, she stepped up into the borning room. Here, close to the warm kitchen hearth, was where the first inhabitants of the house had given birth, nursed the sick, and died. This was where she had put her most prized possession, the curly maple sleigh bed.

Monica pulled back the blue and white hand-woven coverlet and found crisp, white sheets. So, she had left the bed made after all. She paid a quick visit to the bathroom, grateful she'd decided to put off closing the house and draining the pipes. Why had she done that? Had she known on some subconscious level that she would need the house? Shivering, she checked the thermostat and raised it to sixty-eight.

Then she pulled off her shoes, slipped off her slacks, and climbed into the bed, pulling the covers around her shoulders. Involuntarily, she let out a long, shuddering sigh.

She was so tired. Here was where she would rest, lick her wounds, and gather her strength. The house was old; it had endured centuries of nor'east storms, winter blizzards, summer heat waves, and decades of neglect. She had restored it and brought it back to life. Now, it was the old homestead's turn to shelter and protect her. She felt safe here. She reached up and turned off the light. She slept.

CHAPTER ONE

"This place is a firetrap. It ought to be torn down."

Sue Finch bit neatly into a crisp apple, closed her eyes, and raised her face to the warm October sun while she chewed. She was sitting on the ramshackle porch of the Ezekiel Hallett house, once the grandest mansion in Tinker's Cove. Now, it was little more than a decaying pile of tinder.

"How can you say that?" asked her companion, Lucy Stone. She thought of the fantastic tower rising above their heads, the mansard roof, and the fanciful urns that perched on every corner. "It's a fabulous example of Victorian seaside architecture. It ought to be restored."

Lucy spoke softly. She didn't want to disturb six-week-old baby Zoe, who was asleep in the red corduroy baby carrier she wore strapped to her chest.

"As what? It's much too big for a family."

"It could be a restaurant, or an inn. Just look at this view."

From where they sat on the porch the two women could see the little town of Tinker's Cove spread out before them. Low, rocky hills sheltered the harbor where a few Cape Island boats bobbed at anchor off the fish pier. The water was a deep blue today, and the tree covered hills wore their fall colors of red and gold.

"Think of the heating bills," said Sue, pulling her sweater off over her head and shaking out her hair.

"That's new, isn't it?" asked Lucy. "Where'd you get it?"

"At the Carriage Trade," said Sue, naming an expensive specialty shop. "Twenty bucks. Last spring."

"Some people have all the luck," grumbled Lucy. "When I go there all I find is real expensive stuff that I don't have any place to wear. Even if I did find something on sale, I wouldn't know what size to buy. I can't seem to get rid of these extra baby pounds."

"There's a new aerobics studio opening across from the Laundromat. If we weren't so lazy we'd sign up for something. What's the latest? The step, the slide?" said Sue, yawning.

There was a pause in the conversation. The bright sunshine and fresh air, combined with a hearty lunch, was making the women drowsy.

"Are you making Halloween costumes for the kids?" asked Sue.

"No way. Toby's going to wear his werewolf mask and hairy hand gloves from last year. The girls are going as ballerinas—in the tutus they wore in the show last spring."

"They'll freeze," warned Sue.

"I'm having them wear pink tights and turtlenecks underneath. They won't be out too long."

"Is there a party at the church, or the youth center? Something to keep them out of trouble?"

"Not that I know of," said Lucy. "I wish there was. I don't even like them trick-or-treating. You always hear about some maniac who poisoned the candy or put razor blades in the apples. Toby won't go with me and the girls—he wants to go out with his friends. I hope they don't come here. A place like this is a real magnet for kids. Especially on Halloween. Think what could happen if they played with matches, or experimented with cigarettes. It wouldn't take much to burn this place down."

"Like the Hopkins Homestead," said Sue.

"Bill was awfully upset when he heard the news on the radio this morning. That house was his first big project."

Lucy's husband, Bill Stone, was a restoration carpenter.

"That's too bad." Sue was sympathetic. "They said it burned to the ground."

"It did. I drove by on my way to your house. Nothing's left but the chimney. I'm worried Bill's going to take it hard. He really put his heart and soul into that place."

"Is there insurance? Do you think they'll rebuild?" Sue was practical.

"I don't know. Bill tried to call the owners, but there wasn't any answer. He wanted to tell Monica himself, before she heard it on the news or something."

"Her husband's a doctor, right?"

"Yeah. They live near Boston. The house was really her project. Bill said she was the perfect client. Lots of money, and good taste, too."

"A rare combination," said Sue.

Lucy smiled. Zoe was shifting around in the baby carrier and it felt a bit like being pregnant again. She got up on her feet and walked back and forth on the porch, hoping to lull the baby back to sleep.

"Doesn't it seem like we're having an awful lot of fires lately?" she asked, leaning against a post.

"Well, yeah, now that you mention it. There was the old movie theater just after the Fourth of July. It was damaged, but they were able to save it. Winchester College is going to renovate it, turn it into a performing arts center."

"Then there was that barn out on Bumps River Road," said Lucy, sitting down Indian fashion and undoing the carrier straps so Zoe could nurse. "When was that?"

"Mid-August. I remember because I was getting Sidra ready to go back to school." Sue's oldest daughter was a sophomore at Bowdoin.

"Who did that belong to?"

"Nobody. It was listed 'owner unknown' in the tax files."

"And now the Hopkins Homestead."

"Don't forget that fire at the old powder house. They caught it before it did much damage."

"Right." Lucy nodded. The powder house, a tiny relic of the Revolutionary War, stood in Brooks Park. "It's kind of suspicious, isn't it? All these fires?"

"Not really. They were all old buildings, but old buildings are more likely to burn. The wood gets dry." Sue picked off a bit of shingle and it crumbled to dust in her hand. "I'll bet this place is next. Want to take a look inside before it's gone?"

"Can we? Isn't it locked up?"

"I know how to get in." Sue grinned mischievously.

"Okay," said Lucy. "Zoe doesn't seem very hungry." Standing up she rearranged her clothes and refastened the baby carrier. "I'm game if you are."

Hopping off the porch, Sue led the way around to the back of the mansion. Pushing aside some overgrown bushes she revealed a flight of stone steps.

"This is the kitchen entrance. We wouldn't want tradesmen muddying up the front hall."

"Of course not," agreed Lucy, watching closely as Sue pulled off a loose board and opened the door. "You're pretty good at this. How long have you been breaking and entering?"

"Practically my whole life. When I was in high school we used to sneak in here to smoke cigarettes and drink beer."

"I'm shocked," said Lucy, following her friend into the darkness. Zoe's eyes, peeking out over the corduroy carrier, were very large and round.

"This is the kitchen," said Sue, in her best real estate lady voice. "Very roomy."

"It's enormous," said Lucy, glancing around at the cavernous, dungeon like room.

"All the latest in modern appliances," said Sue, waving her arm. "The stove." She pointed to a rusting hulk in one corner. "The dishwasher." Sue indicated a soapstone sink complete with hand pump. "The refrigerator!" Throwing open a pantry door, she sent a startled mouse scurrying for shelter.

"Yuck. Can we go upstairs?"

"This way, madam."

Sue led the way up a flight of surprisingly sturdy wooden steps and opened the door to the dining room. Lucy blinked at the brightness; dusty sunlight streamed through the filthy windows. Long brown ribbons of wallpaper were peeling from the walls, and the carcasses of dead flies crunched under their feet.

"The dining room needs a bit of freshening up," conceded Sue. "The living room is this way, through the hall."

Stepping into the hallway, Lucy paused and let her gaze follow the long curving staircase upward. Long ago the house must have been lovely, and beautiful young ladies in long gowns would have descended these stairs to greet the handsome beaux who waited for them below.

"I see this old place is casting a spell on you," said Sue. "Would you like to see the ballroom?"

"Ballroom?"

"I kid you not." Sue tugged at a pair of warped French doors and finally succeeded in opening them. She bowed with a little flourish as Lucy entered the room.

It was a long, rectangular room with three sets of French doors along one side. There was a magnificent, ornate marble fireplace at one end and a balcony for musicians at the other. Facing the French doors there was a wall of matching mirrors, now spotty and dusty. The panels between the doors were decorated with carved wood shaped into lavish bouquets of flowers. Gilt sconces, long since robbed of their crystals, lined the walls.

"Sue, how can you say you want to see all this demolished?" asked Lucy. "It's fabulous."

"It could be, if somebody had hundreds of thousands of dollars to spend fixing it up. But that's not going to happen. It's been empty for a zillion years, falling apart bit by bit. A rock through a window here, a piece of paneling ripped out there, it's like the death of a thousand cuts. I'm all for a swift mercy killing."

"You really care about this old place."

"They just don't build 'em like this anymore. Hey, I want to show you something."

Returning to the hallway, Sue opened another oak-paneled door and revealed a tiny cabinlike room, barely ten feet square.

"This is the house Ezekiel Hallett was born in. When he got

rich he built the mansion right around his boyhood home. They say he used to come here to get away from his social-climbing wife and daughters."

Lucy examined the rough-sawn plank walls, the packed dirt floor, and the crude hearth.

"This was the entire house?"

"Yup. He was one of seven or eight kids. There's a sleeping loft overhead."

"From this to that," said Lucy, trying to imagine raising a family in such cramped quarters. "It's incredible."

"He did it the hard way—selling guano."

"What is guano, anyway?" asked Lucy, heading for the door. She found the tiny, windowless room claustrophobic. "I'm gonna go out on the porch. I need some air."

"Okay," said Sue. "I'll lock the door behind you and backtrack through the house."

"I forgot. We didn't come in through the front door, did we?"

Lucy stepped outside and busied herself gathering the picnic things. She was struggling to her feet when Sue reappeared.

"You know, Lucy, it might be kind of fun to try out that gym," she suggested.

"I think I'm past help. Besides, I don't have any energy to spare."

"They say working out gives you energy, though I don't quite see how," admitted Sue. "I'll give them a call. See if they've got a good deal."

"Don't forget to ask if they have child care," said Lucy, opening the car door and beginning the process of transferring Zoe from the baby carrier to the car seat.

"I'll call," said Sue, hopping into her little sports car and starting the engine.

Lucy watched as she zoomed down the dirt driveway, disappearing in a swirl of dust. Finally clicking the last strap in place, she looked down at the baby. "Do you think I'm too fat?" she asked.

Zoe folded her hands across her chest, and closed her eyes. She was as inscrutable as a little Buddha.

"Okay, be like that," said Lucy, settling herself behind the steering wheel and turning the key in the ignition.

CHAPTER TWO

Ted Stillings, editor-in-chief, reporter, photographer, and publisher of *The Pennysaver*, parked his aging subcompact in front of the Hopkins Homestead and climbed out.

"Whew," he said, shaking his head. He'd covered a lot of fires in his career, but never one this bad. There was literally nothing left of the house. The massive chimney, now black with soot and surrounded by a mound of charred rubble, was all that remained.

A yellow plastic ribbon encircled the site, and a few curious onlookers stood politely behind it. Inside the cordon, Fire Chief Stan Pulaski stood chatting with Police Chief Oswald Crowley. Ted lifted the yellow ribbon, ducked under it, and approached them.

"Hey, you! Stay behind that line," ordered Crowley. He knew perfectly well who Ted was, but enjoyed being as obnoxious as possible.

"Cut it out, Crowley," yelled Ted. "I need some information."

"You think writing that paper of yours gives you special privileges or something?" Crowley narrowed his eyes, and picked at his yellow teeth with his fingernail.

"People want to know what happened and I want to tell them," said Ted, turning to face Pulaski. "So, Chief, what's the story?"

"I haven't finished the report yet," he answered affably. "Soon as I do you can pick up a copy at the station."

"Thanks." Ted surveyed the scene. "Mind if I take a few pictures?"

"I guess that'll be all right. Stay clear of the debris, okay?"

"Sure."

Ted walked off a short way and pulled his camera out of the worn bag that hung from his shoulder. He busied himself screwing on a lens and adjusting the exposure while keeping one ear cocked. He wasn't above a little discreet eavesdropping.

"Damn reporters," he heard Crowley mutter.

"Better get used to it," advised Pulaski. "This is gonna be a big story, soon as somebody figures out we've had four fires in four months."

Ted looked through the viewfinder and stepped a little closer to the two chiefs.

"He's late." Crowley consulted his watch. "Girl in his office said he'd be here at nine."

"Here he is," announced Pulaski, nodding as an official blue van pulled into the driveway. Neat white letters on the side and back read FIRE MARSHAL.

Ted whistled softly to himself, pulled out his notebook, and joined the two chiefs in greeting the newcomer.

"Mike Rogers, assistant fire marshal," he said with a grin, extending his hand. Rogers was a friendly fellow.

"Ted Stillings, Pennysaver Press," said Ted, shouldering his way between Crowley and Pulaski and grasping his hand. "Have you got Sparky with you?" Ted knew all about Sparky, the accelerant-sniffing dog, from the frequent press releases issued by the state fire marshal's office.

"Sure do. He's right here."

Rogers opened the back door of the van and released the dog, a youthful black Labrador, from his portable wire kennel. Sparky gave an enormous yawn, stretched, shook himself, and waited patiently while his leash was fastened. Then, walking smartly beside his handler, he went to work.

"This dog's been trained to identify more than a hundred different accelerants?" asked Ted, pointedly ignoring Crowley's disapproving glare.

"That's right. He went to a special school in Michigan. I went too. We work as a team."

"Is that right?" asked Ted, scribbling away in his notebook. "Where does Sparky live?"

"He lives with me. He's part of the family. When I go to work, he goes, too."

"Is he a good pet?"

"He's great. My kids love him," said Rogers, pausing at the edge of the debris and scratching the dog's neck. "Okay, the way we do this is we sweep the site in a systematic way, working from the outside in. Don't follow me, Ted. There may be hot spots and I don't want to disturb any evidence."

"So what made you call in the fire marshal, Chief?" Ted threw out the question in a deliberately offhand manner as he peered through the viewfinder. "Is there something suspicious about this fire?"

Crowley and Pulaski exchanged glances.

"It was a very fast, very hot fire. The house was completely engaged in a matter of minutes. That doesn't happen unless there are multiple points of origin." Pulaski took off his peaked cap and wiped his forehead with a large white handkerchief.

"You mean arson?"

"Maybe."

"Crowley, have you got any suspects?" There was a slight challenge in Ted's tone.

"No comment." Crowley's attention was on the dog, who had assumed a classic pointing position. "There?" he called.

"Yup," said Rogers, squatting down and opening a toolbox. As they watched he took a sample of the burned material and carefully placed it in a jar.

Sparky indicated the presence of accelerant in three more locations along what had been the outside wall of the house. Once he began investigating the inside, however, he didn't seem to find anything. The man and the dog worked slowly, stepping gingerly among the blackened boards and other charred remains. Ted had plenty of time to get some dramatic photos of Sparky in action.

Rogers spoke softly to the dog, encouraging him and keeping his mind on his task. They had reached the far side of the house, behind the chimney, when the dog began whining and scratching frantically at the rubble.

"What's he found?" shouted Pulaski, hurrying over. "More accelerant?"

"No." Rogers shook his head. "I'm afraid you've got some human remains here."

"A body?" Crowley was doubtful. "This is just a summer place. Nobody's here after Labor Day."

"He only does this when he finds a body," said Rogers. He glanced at the dog who was standing rigid and shivering.

"There is no body here," insisted Crowley. "I don't see a body. There's nothing but ashes."

"It was a hot fire," Rogers reminded him. "There's probably teeth, bone fragments, maybe even jewelry. I'll have to call in specialists from the medical examiner's office. Meanwhile, let's get this area secured and covered with a tarp."

"Winchell," Crowley yelled to a young officer who was standing nearby. "Find Carter. Get on this right away."

"Okay, Chief," he said, setting off across the yard at a trot.

"I think we're about done here," said Rogers, gently tugging at Sparky's leash and leading the trembling dog back to the van. "Good boy." He stroked the animal behind his ears. Sparky gave him a look of doggy adoration and licked his hand.

"What happens now?" Ted asked the chief. But before Crowley could tell Ted to mind his own business he was interrupted by Winchell.

"Chief, Carter's found a car behind that shed. A BMW."

"Damn," said the chief. The last thing he wanted was a homicide.

"You, Stillings." He stabbed a fat finger at Ted's chest. "I want you out of here." He cocked his thumb. "Now."

"Okay, okay," said Ted, holding his hands up. "I know when I'm not wanted."

He started off toward his car, and Pulaski joined him, walking companionably alongside. Unlike the police chief, Pulaski understood the value of a good working relationship with the local media.

"Check at the station, Ted. We'll be scheduling a press conference this afternoon, tomorrow morning at the latest."

"Thanks."

"No problem." He paused. "I have something to say." Ted got out his pad, and when he was ready, Pulaski continued. "I hate arson. Every time my men go out to fight a fire, they put themselves at risk. Every time. And now we've got a death. Somebody died in this fire.

"This is my pledge to the people of Tinker's Cove: I'm going to catch this bastard. But I need help. Anybody sees any suspicious activity, especially around a vacant building, call us. Call right away. Arson's hard to prove, unless the perpetrator is caught in the act. Got that?"

"Got it."

Humming softly to himself, Ted got behind the wheel of his car. He was already rearranging the front page in his mind. Scratch the photo of the jack-o'-lantern, put the "Healthy Holiday Treats" interview with the school dietitian on page five, move "Officer Culpepper's Rules for a Safe Halloween" to page six. Arson, homicide, this was going to be one hell of a Halloween issue.

CHAPTER THREE

There was an annoying buzz in the room. If she didn't stop it, it would wake up the baby.

Lucy sat up in bed. She opened her eyes. Zoe was sleeping peacefully in her white wicker bassinet. She couldn't find the hum.

"Lucy, turn off the alarm."

"Unh." She reached out and pressed the button. She flopped back on her pillow and felt herself slipping back in the warm cocoon of sleep. So easy to drift off, except for the tug of her conscience. She had to get the kids ready for school, and Bill off to work. She threw off the covers and sat up, groping for slippers and robe. Standing, she staggered slightly and caught her balance on the door frame.

She crossed the hall to her eleven-year-old son's room. Picking her way carefully across the dirty clothes and sports equipment that littered the floor, she gave his shoulder a shake. "Toby, it's time to get up."

Next she stuck her head in Sara and Elizabeth's room. "Good morning, girls," she called. Elizabeth was nine, going on twenty-nine, and Sara was five.

She went down the steep back stairs to the kitchen, made the coffee, and continued on into the downstairs bathroom. She splashed cold water on her face and looked in the mirror. Short black hair stuck out all over her head and there were bags under her eyes. She looked terrible. What did she expect? She'd been up most of the night with the baby. She brushed her teeth.

Back in the kitchen, she poured herself a cup of coffee and sat down at the table, resting her head on her hands.

"Mom, I need you to sign this." Toby's voice pulled her back to consciousness.

"What is it?"

"A pledge that you won't abuse your body by taking any illegal drugs."

"No problem," she mumbled, scribbling her name. "Got any speed, man?"

"What?"

"Nothing." She took a long swallow of coffee.

When she next opened her eyes, she saw Bill standing at the counter, dressed for work in a plaid flannel shirt and jeans, buttering a pile of toast.

"Sara, that pink scrunchy is mine," said Elizabeth.

"No, it isn't." Sara's voice started to climb the scale. "It's mine!"

"Let her wear it," said Lucy.

"That's so unfair. You're always siding with her." Elizabeth stamped across the kitchen and plunked herself down on a chair.

"What's the matter with your eye?" asked Bill, setting a glass of orange juice in front of her.

Lucy squinted suspiciously at Elizabeth. She reached out and ran a finger across her eyelid.

"Eye shadow! Wash it off."

Elizabeth glared at her, then stomped off to the bathroom.

"More coffee?" Bill had the pot ready.

"Please. Intravenously."

"Mom, can you come to school tomorrow?" asked Sara. "Officer Barney is visiting our class." Sara was in kindergarten, and she loved it. After watching Toby and Elizabeth go off to school every day, she was finally in school, too.

"Sure," said Lucy. She looked up as Elizabeth returned. "That looks much better."

"All the other girls wear makeup."

"Right." Lucy heard the roar of the school bus engine, as it began the climb up Red Top Road. "You better get going. The bus will be here any minute."

The kids pushed and shoved, grabbing their backpacks and lunches, then clattered out, slamming the door behind them. Lucy picked herself up and started up the stairs, heading back to bed.

"What the hell?" Bill was peering out the kitchen window, thoughtfully stroking his beard.

Lucy joined him. "Oh, my God," she groaned, spotting a huge old Chrysler Imperial turning into the driveway, narrowly missing a whiskey barrel planted with bronze chrysanthemums. "It's Miss Tilley. What could she want so early in the morning?"

"The old witch probably hasn't been to bed yet," said Bill. "Probably been riding her broomstick all night."

Stifling a yawn, Lucy opened the door. "Miss Tilley, what a nice surprise!"

Like most everyone in Tinker's Cove, Lucy didn't dare address the old woman by her first name. Only a select group of her dearest friends referred to Julia Ward Howe Tilley, the former librarian of the Broadbrooks Free Library, as Julia.

Casting a disapproving glance at Lucy, who found herself involuntarily buttoning up her ratty old velour robe, the old woman wasted no time getting to the point. "Bill, it was really you I came to see," she said, baring her complete set of rather dingy original teeth in a ferocious smile.

"Me?"

"Sit down. I have something I want to discuss. You, too, Lucy."

Meekly, they obeyed, waiting while the old woman settled herself.

"As you know," she began, folding her knobby, arthritic hands together on the edge of the table, "I am a member of the Tinker's Cove Historic District Commission. The chairman, in fact. Unfortunately, we have a vacancy now that Porter Lambkin has resigned. He has cancer and says his treatment will prevent him from attending meetings." From Miss Tilley's expression, it was clear she disapproved. In her eyes, sickness was usually nothing more than a convenient excuse for neglecting one's duty.

"I wouldn't have expected it of him," she fumed. "He's left us in a terrible predicament."

"What do you mean?" asked Lucy.

"Remember when the commission was created? It was supposed to protect the town from tasteless, rampant development. People saw what happened in Freeport, and wanted to make sure that could never happen here. They voted to designate almost all of the town as a historic district, and set up the commission to review all proposals for change within the district. No one who owns property within the district can make any changes without getting a certificate of appropriateness from the commission."

Lucy and Bill knew all about the commission, usually referred to in *The Pennysaver* as the TCHDC. More and more, however, people were calling it the "hysterical commission." While most everyone agreed it was important to preserve the character of the town, they resented having to get official approval whenever they wanted to change the color of the front door.

"I've been on the commission from the beginning, and so has Porter and Hancock Smith. You know Hancock—the president of the Historical Society. And then there was Kitty Slack and Gerald Asquith from the college. Gerald decided not to run for re-election, and, well, you know all about Kitty."

Lucy did. Only a few months had passed since Kitty, a wealthy widow, had jilted her faithful suitor Gerald Asquith and left town unexpectedly, accompanied by a silver fox of a time-share salesman.

"Only three people were on the ballot for two seats, and one of them was Kitty. It was too late to get her name off the ballot so Jock Mulligan and Doug Durning really ran unopposed. We used to have a nice unanimous board, but those two apparently have a different agenda. They will approve anything. It didn't matter while we had Porter, but now that he's gone the commission has been stalemated. Our votes are always tied. We can't even agree on a fifth member to fill in until elections next year. Then I thought of you, Bill."

He shifted uncomfortably in his seat. "Me?"

"You." Sitting with her back to the window, Miss Tilley's white hair glowed angelically. Her blue eyes twinkled. She smiled sweetly. Anyone who didn't know her would think she was a perfectly nice old lady.

"It's positively Machiavellian, if I say so myself," she cackled. "They can't say no to you. You're a restoration carpenter. You have impeccable credentials."

"I'd like to help," said Bill, "but I don't think I have the time."

"Really?" She raised an eyebrow. "And what do you do most evenings?"

Bill squirmed uneasily.

"I bet you watch TV. Mental masturbation, that's what I call it."

Lucy pressed her lips together, to keep from giggling, and looked at Bill.

"There's nothing the matter with TV," he grumbled. "How often does this thing meet?"

"Once a month."

"I guess I can manage that," he agreed. "But I'm warning you, I'll have to vote the way I see fit."

"Of course, you must vote your conscience," she said, laying heavy emphasis on the last word. "Then we'll see you tomorrow night. Seven o'clock at the town hall."

"Tomorrow? That means I'll miss *Seinfeld!*"

Miss Tilley silenced him with a stare. Only one avenue was left. Bill grabbed his lunch box, gave Lucy a peck on the cheek, and hurried out.

"I'm glad you asked him," said Lucy. "He has a lot to offer. It's about time he got involved. He needs something to take his mind off the Hopkins Homestead fire."

"My thoughts exactly," said Miss Tilley, casting an appraising glance at Lucy. "My dear, I hope you'll take a little bit of advice from an old friend. Even a spinster like myself knows you'll never keep a man interested if you let yourself go the way you have."

Lucy ran a hand through her hair, suddenly self-conscious.

Miss Tilley rose. "You're really quite attractive when you make an effort, my dear. Now, I must be off."

Lucy watched from the door as she trotted across the yard and climbed into her huge old Chrysler, a 1974 Imperial. That was some car, thought Lucy, guessing it was nearly ten feet long. A dinosaur of an automobile decked with tons of chrome. She winced as it lurched into gear, and Miss Tilley slowly wrestled it through a three-point turn. Built on the theory that size equals comfort, the designers had given little thought to maneuverability. In this car you didn't avoid obstacles, you ran right over them.

Miss Tilley finally had the car pointed in the right direction, and gave Lucy a little wave before flooring the gas pedal. Lucy wondered if she could actually see over the steering wheel as she careened down the driveway. She never even noticed when she knocked over the mailbox.

Lucy shook her head, and was thinking of slipping back between the sheets for a quick nap when the phone rang.

"Are you okay?" inquired Sue.

"Sure. Why?"

"You sound so groggy. Do you have a cold?"

"No. Zoe didn't sleep much last night."

"Six-week growth spurt?"

"Probably."

"Listen, Lucy. I had a great idea. I want to have a big Halloween party for the whole town in the Hallett House. Whaddya think?"

"Sounds like fun. Will the fire chief let you do it?"

"I just got off the phone with him. He said he'll issue a temporary occupancy permit if we clean the place up and it passes his inspection."

Hearing a cry from upstairs, Lucy was distracted.

"What? I think I hear Zoe."

"Listen, Lucy, will you help with the party?"

Zoe's cries were coming more frequently, threatening to become a full-blown wail. "Sure. What can I do?"

"Cupcakes?"

Zoe was now screaming, and Lucy could feel her breasts tingle as her milk let down. All she could think of was the baby. "Sure. No problem. How many?"

"Twelve dozen?"

"Okay. I gotta go. Bye." Lucy slammed the earpiece onto the hook, hiked up her long flannel nightie and robe, and started up the stairs taking them two at a time. "Hang on, baby! Mommy's coming!"

CHAPTER FOUR

"What's all the fuss about?" crooned Lucy, bending over the bassinet. Zoe's face was red with rage; she was in no mood for small talk. "I bet you want your breakfast," said Lucy. She scooped up the baby and perched on the side of the bed, offering her breast.

Zoe took it greedily, and began sucking energetically. Feeling herself beginning to relax, Lucy considered falling back on to the pillows, but Zoe was having none of that. She suddenly pulled her head away, leaving Lucy to clamp a diaper over her spraying milk ducts. Lucy tickled the baby's cheek with her milky nipple, but Zoe wasn't interested. She had a soaking wet diaper, and knew perfectly well that it was time for a change and a bath. Lucy knew it, too, but had hoped to postpone it for a bit.

"You're so . . . conservative," she said, placing the baby on her shoulder. "If it's eight-thirty, it must be bath-time."

In the kitchen, Lucy propped Zoe in her plastic baby seat and set it on the counter. She flipped on the radio and began loading the breakfast dishes into the dishwasher. She gave the counter a quick wipe, lined the big porcelain sink with a hand towel, and began filling it with warm water.

Cocking an ear to the radio for the morning news, she gave Zoe a big smile, tickled her tummy, and eased her out of her rather damp terry suit. Removing the wet diaper, she slipped the naked baby into the water.

Cradling her head in the crook of her arm, Lucy listened to the Oil Peddler promise 24-hour delivery as she gently splashed water on Zoe's round tummy.

"Regular exercise can make you look and feel better," advised a feminine voice.

"That's right," said Lucy, nodding and smiling at the baby. At six weeks, she was looking less like a newborn and more like a real baby. Her little limbs were no longer folded tight against her torso. "You love to exercise, don't you? You love to wave those arms and kick those legs."

"My name is Krissy Wright," continued the voice, "and I'm inviting you to stop by my new exercise studio, the Body Shop, for a free introductory class."

"Shall we do that? Would you like to work out? Oh!" said Lucy in surprise, as Zoe splashed her in the face. Zoe gave a little chuckle, and smiled.

"Is that a smile?" cooed Lucy, returning the gesture.

Zoe's eyes were fixed intently on her mother's face, and she smiled again.

"Definitely a smile," crowed Lucy. "Aren't you a smart little girl!"

Zoe agreed, and flapped her arm rhythmically in the water, startling herself with the resulting splash. Before she could cry, Lucy distracted her by singing along with the radio. "Hey, where ya goin? I'm goin' to the Lobster Bar, 'cause that's where the best . . . lobsters are!"

Lucy hummed along with the radio as she quickly soaped Zoe's silky, tiny body, and rinsed her off, then wrapped her in a fluffy towel. With the baby propped against her shoulder, she waltzed around the kitchen gathering the diapering supplies.

Spreading the towel beneath her, she laid Zoe down on the kitchen table. Whenever Lucy saw her like that, naked and helpless, she felt a little stab of fear. So many things could happen to a baby. Just last night she had watched a TV news segment about a dangerous cradle. Nine unwary mothers had tucked their babies in for the night only to find them dead in the morning.

Then there was her own private nightmare, in which she drove off on an errand and forgot the baby. She'd dreamt it often since coming home from the hospital, and always woke up in a panic. Then, she wouldn't be able to get back to sleep until she checked the bassinet and made sure Zoe was safe. After four babies one wouldn't expect these irrational fears to keep popping up, but they did.

"You babies sure know how to drive mommies crazy, yes you do," crooned Lucy, pulling a clean diaper out of the basket of unsorted laundry in the corner. "I'm crazy over you," she sang along with a popular tune, snapping the diaper cover firmly in place. She was just tucking Zoe's arms and legs into a stretchy little suit, when the music ended and the announcer read the news tease.

"Police say a suspicious Tinker's Cove fire claimed the life of at least one victim. More in a moment."

"Oh, no," she muttered, as she settled herself in the rocking chair. As Zoe nuzzled her chest, now eager for a late breakfast, Lucy wondered who the victim could have been.

It couldn't have been any of the Mayes, she assured herself. The family only used the house in the summer. Perhaps it was a vagrant or homeless person who had broken into the empty house looking for a night's shelter.

"Please, please don't let it be one of the kids," she sent up a little prayer. There wasn't much to do in Tinker's Cove, and Toby's friends sometimes did things they shouldn't. Exciting and forbidden things, like entering someone's deserted summer cottage.

Lucy began to nurse, gently stroking her baby's downy head. She bent down and sniffed Zoe's clean baby scent. It was the best smell in the world. Just then the announcer's voice interrupted her reverie.

"The fire that destroyed the Hopkins Homestead early Tuesday morning also claimed the life of its owner, Monica Mayes. Remains found at the site by state fire investigators have been positively identified by the medical examiner."

Lucy sat motionless as Zoe continued her rhythmic sucking. It took a minute for the information to sink in. Gradually, grief engulfed her and tears ran down her face.

"No, not Monica," she whispered.

"This means we are no longer investigating a case of arson," Lucy recognized Police Chief Oswald Crowley's voice, in a recorded sound bite. "This is now a homicide investigation."

Homicide? Who would want to kill Monica? She remembered Monica laughing, recounting how an inept young traffic cop had tied up traffic for miles on Route 1, by stopping the line of cars for every pedestrian who wanted to cross the street. They'd been standing outside, and Monica's coppery hair had blazed in the sun.

Lucy thought of the flames, flickering brightly as they consumed the Homestead.

She remembered Monica flipping through wallpaper books, determined to find exactly the right paper for the bathroom, and her excitement when Bill showed her the 1703 penny that had been placed under the threshold to guarantee prosperity.

Lucy thought of her husband, busy at another old house. He had been so fond of Monica, just as she had. He shouldn't hear this on the radio. She ought to tell him.

Zoe was asleep in her arms. Lucy knew she would sleep soundly for a couple of hours. She carried her upstairs and tucked her in the bassinet, then quickly showered and dressed herself.

An hour later, steering her little silver Subaru wagon along the back roads with Zoe securely fastened in the safety seat, Lucy thought of Monica.

She had been one of Bill's first clients, and initially had seemed to be just another pampered, rich doctor's wife who wanted a summer place that would impress her city friends. When they first discussed the restoration of the Homestead, Bill had come prepared with estimates for alarm systems, air-conditioning, even a Jacuzzi tub.

"I don't know," Monica had said doubtfully, shaking her head. "This is a very old house. Somehow these things don't seem to belong. I know we can't be one hundred percent authentic, after all, this isn't 1703 and I don't want to use an outhouse! But I'd like this to be a place where we live simply, and get back to the basics, know what I mean?"

Bill had nodded.

"What about your husband?" Lucy had asked. "Men don't like to give up their gadgets."

"He says he wants to make a woodpile." Monica shrugged. "I'm not sure he knows how. He's a gynecologist." She changed the subject. "This means so much to me. I've always wanted to have an old house."

At first, Lucy had been a little jealous of Monica. She had money and social status, and although older than Lucy, was still extremely attractive. Her skin was nourished and revitalized, her hair was highlighted and carefully coiffed, and she was a living testament to the benefits of regular exercise.

At the time, Lucy was struggling through the first months of her pregnancy with Toby, and she felt bloated and nauseous. Lucy was pretty sure that if Monica had given Bill the least encouragement, he would have hopped into bed with her.

But she never had. She'd become a friend to both of them. She'd become Bill's eager student, listening carefully as he explained the old construction methods. She insisted that he do what he thought best for the house and refused to cut corners to save money. As a result, the house had been one of Bill's most satisfying projects, and he was justifiably proud of the work he did there.

She took Lucy along to country auctions, and together they learned how to tell the treasures from the trash. When Lucy fell in love with a golden oak high chair, but was quickly outbid by a dealer, Monica noted the buyer's identity. She bought the chair from him, and surprised Lucy with it as a baby gift.

That was the sort of person she was. She quickly became involved in people's lives, and showered them with affection. Always quick to smile and laugh, revealing those pearly white teeth.

Did they use her teeth to identify her? Lucy wondered, with a stab of pain. Had Monica been quietly overcome by smoke in her sleep, or had she woken in a panic realizing the house was on fire? Had she found the doorway blocked by flames, and struggled to open a window? What were her last moments like? Had she been afraid? Had she suffered?

Lucy couldn't bear to think about it. She wanted to remember Monica as she'd been. A beautiful woman who loved life.

How was she going to tell Bill? How could she soften the impact? Bill wasn't the sort of man who expressed his deepest emotions openly, but Lucy knew he'd taken the fire very hard. He hadn't said much, but she knew he was simmering with anger. As she pulled the Subaru up next to Bill's truck and braked, Lucy felt heavy with the weight of the terrible news she had to deliver.

CHAPTER FIVE

Moving automatically, Lucy opened the car door and got out. She pulled open the rear door and reached in to loosen the straps that held the baby seat. Bracing herself, she awkwardly lifted the cumbersome plastic shell that held the baby. Then she climbed the makeshift steps and entered the spacious hall of the Hathorn-Pye house. The house had recently been purchased by the Maine Museum of Fine Arts, and Bill had been hired to restore it.

"Bill?" she called.

"I'm in here," he answered. Lucy followed his voice and found him bent over a window frame in one of the front rooms.

"This is a nice surprise," he said, looking up.

"Zoe was restless," improvised Lucy, trying to ease her way into breaking the news, "so I took her for a drive." She set down the heavy baby seat, and tucked a shawl around the sleeping baby.

"I thought you'd be back in bed."

"I wish I was," she confessed, crossing the room to stand beside him. "Sue called and the phone woke the baby. Wotcha doin'?"

"Taking a paint sample, so I can figure out the original color."

"This is a lovely house," observed Lucy, looking around. "I love the proportions."

"It's a classic Georgian," said Bill. "The museum was smart to buy it. They got it for a song. It's a fine house, Captain Hathorn spared no expense when he built it. It was his statement to the world that he had arrived." Bill began carefully dismantling the window frame.

"I love the big front hall, and those stairs."

"That hallway told visitors the captain had money to waste on space that wasn't needed for cooking or sleeping."

"I wonder what the captain's wife was like," mused Lucy.

"Which one?" asked Bill, carefully prying off a piece of window casing. "The first three all died in childbirth, not one lived past twenty-five. The fourth was a rich old widow who already had six children."

"My goodness," said Lucy, recalled to her grim task. "Bill, I've got some bad news. Terrible news."

He straightened up and turned to face her.

"Monica was there," said Lucy, her voice breaking. "She died in the fire."

He shook his head, refusing to believe her. "It must have been somebody else. A vagrant or something. Monica was never there except in the summer."

"She was there. They've identified her." Tears were now running down her face.

"Where did you hear this?" Bill's voice was sharp.

"On the radio."

His face went white and slack; he looked as if he'd been kicked in the stomach. Then his jaw tightened and he turned away, facing the wall. Raising his fist, he slammed it against the tough old horsehair plaster, raising a cloud of dust.

Lucy reached up and touched his shoulder. He spun around and drew her against him, burying his face in her hair. They clung together for a long time. Finally, he pulled himself away and began to pace.

"Dammit," he said, suddenly stricken with guilt. "It was my fault. There was no smoke alarm in that house. They changed the code a year or two later. If I'd thought to put one in she might have lived. At least she would have had a chance to get out."

"It's not your fault. You did everything you were supposed to. She was just in the wrong place at the wrong time."

"Damn. I hate fires."

"I know," said Lucy, thinking once again of the flames, remorselessly consuming everything and leaving only ashes. And bones. She shivered. "Do you want to take the day off? We could go for a ride or something—something to take our minds off the fire." She wiped her face with a crumpled tissue she'd found in her pocket.

"Thanks," he said, gently caressing her shoulder. "I'd rather work. I've got some old ceiling tile upstairs that has to come down. Today seems like a good day to rip a building apart."

"Just be sure you stop with the ceiling tile," said Lucy, attempting a feeble joke. "I don't want you to tear down the whole place."

"I'm not guaranteeing anything," said Bill, pulling a crowbar out of his toolbox and picking up the battered old tape player he kept on the job. "You'd better get out of here if you don't want Zoe to wake up. I'm gonna play some AC/DC—real loud."

"Be careful," cautioned Lucy. "We don't need any broken bones."

"See ya later," he said, mounting the stairs.

Back in the car, heading for home, Lucy could think of nothing but the fires. Sue was wrong. These fires weren't just happening. She was sure someone was setting them. But who? What sort of person would do such a thing? Did he stand in the dark, watching as the flames grew stronger, listening for the wail of the sirens? Why did he do it? Was he frightened, now that someone had died? Or was he thrilled by the fact that he had taken a human life? Would Monica's death spur him on to set more fires?

Pulling into her driveway, Lucy regarded her own comfortable home. A spacious white clapboard farmhouse, it had been built in the 1850s, just before the Civil War. The builder was known to have had strong abolitionist sympathies, and some people believed the house had been a stop on the Underground Railroad.

Lucy loved her house. She loved the fact that it was old, and the thought of the many generations it had sheltered reassured her. To her the house was a tangible link to the past, and a launching pad for the future. More than a wedding ring, or a big diamond, it was proof of the commitment she and Bill had made to each other. The house had been in terrible shape when they bought it, a real handyman's special, and they had labored together to make it a home.

We could be next, she thought, feeling very vulnerable. The house, after all, was nothing but wood. Mostly old wood. Like the others, it would go up in a flash We're not safe. Nobody's safe, she thought, nobody who lives in an old house.

She shifted into park, switched off the engine, and began to unfasten the straps that held Zoe in the safety seat. Still sound asleep, Zoe didn't even blink. Lucy gazed at her beautiful baby and gently stroked her cheek. What if their house began to burn like the Hopkins Homestead? Would she be able to save Zoe?

She didn't want to find out. Whoever was setting the fires, this maniac, had to be found and stopped.

CHAPTER SIX

"Never, ever eat any of your trick or treat candy before your parents have a chance to look it over."

The next morning, Lucy kept her promise to Sara and visited the kindergarten. As she joined the other mothers in the back of the room, she felt remarkably light and unencumbered without the baby carrier strapped to her chest. She had taken Sue at her word when she insisted she would be happy to baby-sit and had left Zoe with her.

Lucy always enjoyed visiting the elementary school. Here, in the brightly decorated rooms, order prevailed. The children marched in lines, two by two. They practiced their round letters on lined paper. The answers were right, or they were wrong. There was none of the conflict and confusion that reigned in the real world. Here, for just a few minutes anyway, she could push the fire and Monica's death to a dark, back corner of her mind.

Catching Officer Barney Culpepper's eye, she gave him a little wave. He was standing in the front of the room, surrounded by the entire kindergarten class who were sitting cross-legged on the floor. At six feet, with a stocky build, he seemed enormous compared to the children. Lucy looked for Sara and found her in the front row, next to her best friend, Jenn Baker.

A hand shot up, and Culpepper leaned forward.

"Joey Wade, do you have a question?"

"What if my mom eats all my candy?"

The question set off a chorus of anxious laughter; Joey had voiced a shared concern.

"If you ate all your trick or treat candy yourself you'd probably get an enormous stomachache," said Culpepper, grabbing his beer belly and groaning. "I hate it when that happens, don't you?"

The kids laughed and nodded, and a few of the more active boys imitated him, grabbing their stomachs and groaning.

"John, Peter." The names were accompanied by a stern look from teacher Lydia Volpe, and the boys settled down. Lydia was a pro, she had been teaching for years. She had also taught Toby and Elizabeth.

"There's a reason why your parents should check your candy. They want to make sure it's okay for you to eat, that it hasn't been opened, and there are no germs." Officer Culpepper was doing his best to warn the kids without frightening them, thought Lucy.

"My cousin got an apple for Halloween and he bit into it and there were pins inside," volunteered a blond little girl dressed all in pink.

"My cousin bit into an apple and there was a razor blade," added a little brunette, already accomplished in the art of one-upmanship.

A general buzz ensued in which Lucy heard poison, thumbtacks, and broken glass mentioned. She was shocked. Where did five-year-olds hear these things?

"Now, children," reminded Mrs. Volpe. "Officer Culpepper hasn't finished. He has more to tell us." Her dark eyes flashed. "We listen with our ears, not our mouths."

"Some of the stories you hear about Halloween aren't true," advised the policeman. "But it's better to be safe than sorry." He turned the page of an oversized flip chart. "These are my safety tips for Halloween. Number one: Never go trick or treating alone. Who are you going with, Joey?"

"My brother."

"That's good. How about you, Heather?"

"With my mom."

"And you, Billy?"

"I don't know yet."

"Well, be sure you don't go alone," said Culpepper. "Here's tip number two: Don't wear a mask that covers your eyes and makes it hard to see. What can you use, if you're not wearing a mask? Samantha?"

"Makeup?" Samantha was enchanted with the idea.

"That's right. Makeup is better than a mask. Now for tip number three. If you go out after dark, carry a flashlight. Why should you carry a flashlight, Billy?"

"So you can see where you're going?"

"You got it. And so the drivers of cars can see you. Ready for tip number four? Here it comes. You've heard it before. Have your parents check your candy before you eat it. Only one tip left. Sara, can you guess what it is?"

"You shouldn't smash pumpkins or throw eggs or things like that," said Sara, nodding virtuously. She obviously remembered an unfortunate incident last Halloween, when Toby had been caught toilet-papering the principal's hedge. Lucy felt a blush rising from her turtleneck and studied her shoes as her cheeks reddened.

"That's very true," agreed Culpepper, winking at Lucy. "Trick or treating is more fun if you leave out the tricks." He flipped to the last page, where a glowing jack-o'-lantern had the letters HAVE FUN carved into its face. "Tip number five is to have fun. Everybody, what are you going to do on Halloween?" he asked.

"Have fun!" the children chorused back.

"Thank you, Officer Culpepper, for visiting our class," said Mrs. Volpe in her teacher's voice. "Class, how do we thank Officer Culpepper?"

"Thank you, Officer Culpepper," they shouted in unison.

"We have a Halloween treat for Officer Culpepper and our other visitors today," announced Mrs. Volpe. "If Officer Culpepper will go to the back of the room with the others, the children can stand in the front."

Culpepper joined the handful of mothers in the back of the room, placing himself next to Lucy, while Mrs. Volpe quickly arranged the children in front of the blackboard. "First, we have a finger-play. Ready?" The children raised their hands in front of their faces. "Begin."

"Five little pumpkins sitting on a gate," chanted the children.

"The first one said." They each raised a finger. "My, it's getting late."

"The second one said." Another finger went up. "I hear a noise."

"The third one said." Three fingers were now up. "It's only some boys."

"The fourth one said." Only the thumbs were folded. "Having Halloween fun."

"The fifth one said." Out popped the thumbs. "Let's run, let's run!"

"When, OOH went the wind, and OUT (here they all clapped) went the lights, and away they all RAN (the hands went behind their backs) on Halloween night!"

The mothers applauded, smiling and beaming with pride.

"Now for our song." Mrs. Volpe clapped her hand once and the children began singing to the tune of "Frere Jacques."

"Pumpkin moonshines, pumpkin moonshines,
Where are you? Where are you?
Here I am this evening.
Boo, boo, boo! Boo, boo, boo!"

The mothers all laughed and clapped enthusiastically. Lucy caught Sara's eye and gave her a wave and a smile.

"That's the end of our program, thank you for coming," said Mrs. Volpe, indicating the door.

Leaving the room, Lucy walked down the corridor with Officer Culpepper. They had been friends for a long time, and they'd gotten to know each other when they had served together on the Cub Scout Pack Committee.

"So, Barney, what can you tell me about the fire?" asked Lucy.

"Not much," he said, smoothing back his hair and setting his cap on his head. "The chief's taking this kinda personal. He likes to think he's got a quiet, law-abiding town. The fires are bad enough, but now that nice lady Mrs. Mayes got herself killed. He's doubled nighttime patrols—we've got two cruisers out instead of one—and he's got the state troopers helping out. But arson's tough. You can't prove anything unless you catch 'em in the act. We don't have enough manpower to cover every building in town."

"Come on, Barney. That's the official line. I want to know what you really think."

"Trouble is, nobody thought too much about it at first. Just figured it was kids."

"You don't anymore?"

"Nope. School started for one thing. Vandalism always drops once they go back to school. Don't have as much time to get into trouble. Fires oughta stopped, but they didn't. If anything, they've been coming closer together. The frequency is increasing."

"What does that mean?"

"It means we've probably got a nut on our hands. A pyro."

"That's what I think," said Lucy. "And he seems to go for old buildings. It makes me nervous. After all, our house is pretty old."

"I wouldn't worry too much. Guy from the fire marshal's office said he thinks we'll get this nut pretty soon. The more fires he sets the more likely he is to get careless. He'll make a mistake and we'll catch him."

"Somehow that doesn't make me feel a whole lot better. How many fires is it going to take? And it won't bring Monica back."

"That was a real shame," said Barney, holding the door for her.

"It sure was. See you around, Barney."

Lucy paused on the steps and watched as Barney climbed in his cruiser and pulled out of the school driveway. The holiday program hadn't taken long, it was only ten o'clock. There was no need for her to hurry back; Sue wouldn't mind keeping Zoe a bit longer. Making up her mind, Lucy crossed the street to the Broadbrooks Free Library.

The library had changed quite a bit since Miss Tilley's retirement. The polished wood floors that creaked whenever anyone moved, earning the transgressor a baleful stare from Miss Tilley, had been covered with carpet. Fluorescent lights had been installed, and it was now possible to read the titles in the stacks; readers no longer had to guess which was the right book and then take it to the window to check the title. These changes were all instigated by Miss Tilley's successor, perky little Bitsy Howell.

"My replacement" as Miss Tilley insisted on calling her, was breezy and casual. While Miss Tilley had emphasized order, and tolerated nothing out of place, Bitsy thrived on chaos. Her office was a mess, overflowing with papers and books waiting to be cataloged.

Bitsy greeted everyone who came in the door cheerfully, waived overdue fines with abandon, and resolutely ignored the three-book limit. Under her management, circulation had dramatically increased, donations were up, and a building drive was underway.

"Lucy, I haven't seen you for a while. We have some wonderful new children's books—I'm sure Sara would love them."

"I'll have to bring her in," promised Lucy. "I'm doing some research today. Tell me, do you keep old copies of *The Pennysaver?*"

"Sure do. All the way back to 1837. It was called the *Advertiser* in those days. Fascinating reading, if you've got the time."

"I'm only interested in some recent issues. The last few months."

"Sure. They're right here," said Bitsy, ushering Lucy into a workroom. "I'll just move these out of your way," she said, scooping up some magazines, "and you can sit right here. The most recent papers are in this box—we send them to be microfilmed at the end of the year. You're welcome to help yourself, just put them back the way you found them, okay?"

Pulling out a stack, Lucy thumbed through the old newspapers until she found the July 9 issue. Her eye immediately fell on the dramatic page one photo of the old movie theater, which had gone up in flames on Sunday, July 5, providing a fiery climax to the holiday weekend.

Ted's story emphasized the heroism of the firefighters, who had managed to save much of the grand old movie palace. Winchester College had been planning to restore the gilded walls, red plush seats, and ceiling murals to create a performing arts center.

"We're grateful to the wonderful volunteer firefighters," said College President Gerald Asquith. "This terrible fire has delayed the restoration project, but we plan to go forward as soon as additional funds are raised."

There was no suggestion that the fire had been deliberately set. Everyone Ted interviewed agreed the fire was an unfortunate tragedy, probably due to a faulty electrical connection, or perhaps a holiday firework that landed on the wood-shingled roof.

Flipping through the papers, Lucy soon found the story about the second fire. BARN BURNS, blared the headline of the August 28 issue, nearly two months after the first fire. This time, firemen were unable to save the building.

"The structure was fully involved when we arrived," Fire Chief Stanley Pulaski was quoted as saying. "A decision was made not to put any of our personnel at risk, our objective was simply to confine the fire and let it burn itself out."

In other words, thought Lucy, they watched it burn. Again, there was no hint that the fire might have been deliberately set. Spontaneous combustion of new hay was given as the likely cause.

The third fire occurred only a month later, in late September. Fortunately, when the old powder house went up in flames it was quickly discovered, and the antique building, which dated from the Revolutionary War was saved. As Barney suggested, this fire was blamed on youthful vandals.

"I want to make one thing absolutely clear," warned Police Chief Oswald Crowley. "This sort of destructive behavior will not be tolerated in Tinker's Cove."

His warning went unheeded, thought Lucy, grimly noting that the Homestead burned barely three weeks later. This time there was no doubt that the fire was set. ARSON CLAIMS LIFE! declared the headline of the most recent issue. The headline was printed above a stark photo of the Homestead chimney, all that was left after the fire.

The story went on to say that fire officials were now taking a second look at the earlier fires, which seemed in retrospect to be the handiwork of the same deranged individual. "We're determined to catch this perpetrator before he takes any more lives," proclaimed Chief Pulaski.

A related story chronicled the amazing feats of Sparky, the accelerant-sniffing dog. "He's not just my pet," his handler was quoted as saying. "He's my partner."

As she replaced the papers in a neat pile, Lucy recited the dates of the fires. July 5. August 28. September 26. October 19. There didn't seem to be a pattern to the fires, except for the fact that they were coming closer together.

Leaving the workroom, Lucy wandered over to the nonfiction section. There, among the self-help books she found a thick volume on abnormal psychology. A glance at the index revealed an entire chapter devoted to "Pyromania and Related Disorders."

Bitsy smiled brightly as Lucy approached the desk.

"That's really heavy reading," she joked, taking the hefty volume. "Sure I can't interest you in something lighter? We have some brand new mysteries."

"I don't have much time to read anymore with the baby. I'm just doing a bit of research."

"We have some excellent material on postpartum depression," offered Bitsy, determined to be helpful.

"I'm fine, really," said Lucy. "Just curious about something."

Bitsy couldn't resist. "Curiosity killed the cat. Now, why do people say that? Curiosity is wonderful, isn't it?"

"Sometimes. Sometimes it gets you in trouble." Lucy took the book and tucked it under her arm. She knew from experience that asking questions could be dangerous.

Not this time, she thought, as she left the library and headed for Sue's house. She was determined to find out who was setting the fires, but, she promised herself, she was going to be careful. Very careful.

Besides, she didn't really have enough time to get into too much trouble. Before she started investigating, she had to bake some cupcakes. How many had she promised Sue? Two dozen?

CHAPTER SEVEN

"*Twelve* dozen? I said I'd bake twelve dozen cupcakes? I must have been out of my mind." Lucy was sitting at the huge scrubbed pine harvest table in Sue's kitchen. Sue was always remodeling her kitchen—it had gone from cluttered country to fifties kitsch and now had a definite English accent. A plate rack hung near the sink, a Welsh cupboard hugged one wall, and a cobalt blue Aga stove was her pride and joy.

"You were kind of distracted," admitted Sue. "Forget it. Two dozen will be fine."

"Oh, no," said Lucy. "I'll manage." She knew she owed Sue a favor for taking care of Zoe, and she wanted to even the score as soon as possible. "Did the baby give you much trouble?"

"No. She's a little angel," said Sue. "She fussed a little bit when she realized I wasn't her mommy, she tried the bottle and didn't like it, and gave up and went to sleep. It's a shame to wake her—want some lunch?"

"Sure," said Lucy.

"I've got some leftover Cornish pasties."

"Sounds great," said Lucy, who hadn't the faintest idea what a Cornish pasty was, but was always hungry.

"That was terrible about Monica, wasn't it?" said Sue, popping the meat pies into the microwave.

"I'm still having trouble believing it really happened," admitted Lucy. "What was she doing at the house this time of year, anyway? She only came in the summer." Lucy looked away, staring out the window.

"She had kids, didn't she?"

"All grown up, thank goodness." Lucy's voice quavered, and Sue quickly changed the subject.

"I called the Body Shop. They do have child care, and we can take one free class to try it out. Whaddya say we go over after lunch?"

"Today?"

"Sure," said Sue, slipping a steaming plate in front of Lucy. "These things are full of carbohydrates and fat grams and I don't know what all. Positively deadly."

"Delicious," said Lucy, savoring a mouthful.

An hour later, with Zoe safely installed in the child care center at the Body Shop, Lucy was calculating her chances of surviving the "Basic Body" class.

"Now that's five, and four, and only three more," said the perky blond instructor. They had been at this for forty-five minutes and Vicki had never stopped smiling, never stopped bouncing. Lucy had never seen anyone so completely fit—even Vicki's ponytail was perfectly conditioned. "Okay, now it's time to cool down. Take a deep breath. In, hold it, and out. That's right. Doesn't that feel good?"

Lucy stared at her reflection in the mirror that covered the wall. No doubt about it, she definitely needed this. She had borrowed an old leotard from Sue, and the tight spandex revealed a doughy stomach, flabby arms and thighs. Even her face was puffy. How had this happened? She used to have so much energy, she used to run miles every week. Now, it was all she could do to get up the stairs. And truth be told, she was still wearing her maternity clothes because her old things didn't fit. She either had to get back in shape or buy a whole new wardrobe.

"Okay, ladies, you're done. Now, don't you feel great?"

Lucy laid back on the wood floor, trying to find the energy to get up.

"Come on, lazybones," said Sue, extending a hand. She looked fresh as ever, much to Lucy's disgust.

Lucy took Sue's hand and pulled herself to her feet. Her legs felt wobbly underneath her. But, standing in the shower a few minutes later, she had to admit she felt better than she had in a long time. As the hot water poured over her tired body, soothing her aches and pains, she was aware of herself in a new way. There were muscles under that flab. She decided to sign-up for a membership.

Refreshed and dressed, checkbook in hand, she approached the front desk.

"Hi, I'm Krissy. May I help you?" asked another bright blonde, displaying a dazzling smile.

"I'd like to sign up for the introductory special," said Lucy, glancing at a banner hanging on the brick wall.

"Super! You won't be sorry—it's an investment in yourself. Now, if you'll just fill out this form . . . sorry, I better get that phone." She slipped a sheet of paper in front of Lucy, handed her a pen, and picked up the phone, all in one smooth motion.

Lucy began filling in the blanks, while Krissy took the call.

"Body Shop . . . where fitness is fun. Oh, hi." From the change in tone, Lucy guessed this was someone special.

"What news? I've been so busy with opening the studio that I haven't had time to read the paper or anything. A fire?"

Curious, Lucy glanced at Krissy in time to see an expression of satisfaction flicker across her features. Then, she heard her murmur, "I just can't believe it. I'm so sorry. I'm here for you, you know that."

Krissy hung up the receiver and turned her attention to Lucy. "Sorry about that—my business partner just lost his wife. In a fire. Absolutely awful."

"That's too bad. It wasn't Monica Mayes, was it?"

"Did you know her?" Krissy's eyebrows shot up in surprise.

"A little," said Lucy.

"Of course. Everybody knows everybody in a town like this. I'm not used to it—I'm from the city. Now, that'll be twenty-nine dollars, and the membership is good for a month. You can take any regularly scheduled classes, use the showers. There is an extra charge for sessions with a personal trainer, massage, things like that. Child care is included. Any questions?"

"No," said Lucy, handing over her check. She was struck by the sudden change in Krissy's attitude. The smile was gone and she was all business. Lucy wondered if she was imagining it, or if Krissy really couldn't wait to get rid of her.

Turning to go toward the nursery, she saw Sue coming out of the dressing room.

"This was a good idea—I got a membership," she said, flashing her brand-new card. "How about you?"

"Me? I'm going to think it over. I'm not sure exercise is for me." Sue puckered her face with distaste and lowered her voice. "It made me sweat."

"That's the point. You're supposed to sweat."

"Oh." Sue tapped her pearly pink lips with a perfectly manicured finger, polished to match, then tucked a lock of her shining black Dutch-boy hair behind one ear. "I'd like to keep you company, Lucy, but I don't really think I have the time. I'll let you know."

Lucy watched as her friend hurried out the door. If Sue wasn't so nice, it would be easy to hate her. She always looked terrific, and she never gained a pound no matter how much she ate. Lucy shook her head and gave a little shrug, then headed for the nursery to retrieve Zoe. She didn't think Sue would have to think it over for very long—she seemed to have already made up her mind.

CHAPTER EIGHT

A tapping at the kitchen door startled Lucy. Exhausted by the workout, she had been dozing in Bill's recliner chair. The psychology book lay on the floor, where it had fallen. She rubbed her eyes and stretched, then hurried to the door. She blinked in surprise, recognizing Monica's husband.

Dr. Roland Mayes was the sort of man who always wore a suit and tie, and looked uncomfortable in casual clothes. On his infrequent visits to Tinker's Cove his polo shirts were obviously brand new, straight out of the package, and his casual slacks were crisply creased. Today, however, Roland didn't look band-box fresh. His suit was rumpled as if he'd worn it for several days, and he had a dark five o'clock shadow.

"Come in, come in," said Lucy. She gave him her best smile, hoping he wouldn't realize how desperately she wished he hadn't come. She had never liked him very much. On the rare occasions when she had spoken with him she had gotten the distinct impression that she was boring him. But now, she told herself, the poor man was bereaved. She had a duty to try and comfort him.

"Take a seat," invited Lucy.

Roland staggered slightly as he headed for the chair, causing Lucy to look at him more closely. His face was pasty gray; he looked as if he was going to faint.

"When did you eat last?"

"I don't remember," he said, sitting down heavily at the table and placing a package in front of him. "I'm not hungry."

"You have to eat," she said. "You need to keep up your strength. How about a sandwich?"

"I could use that," he said. Lucy busied herself mixing up some tuna fish and laying slices of bread out on the counter.

"Bill and I both want you to know how sad we are about Monica," said Lucy. Once again, tears were welling up in her eyes. Fortunately, she had her back to him and was able to brush them away. It wouldn't do to inflict her own grief on this unfortunate man.

"It never should have happened," he said, shaking his head as Lucy set a plate and mug of tea in front of him. "Tuna salad," he said, looking up. "I haven't had this in years."

"Tuna's a staple around here," said Lucy, taking a sip of her own tea. "I suppose you've been to see the police and all. Are they making any progress in the investigation?"

"None, none at all," he answered, taking a bite of his sandwich. "They're absolute incompetents as far as I can tell. I've lost my house, and my wife, and they don't seem to care." His tone was belligerent, almost angry.

"I'm sure that's not true," said Lucy, in a soothing voice.

"Then why did that idiot police chief, Growley or Crowley or whatever his name is, keep me waiting forty-five minutes before he'd see me? And then he gave me the brush-off." Outrage burned in his eyes.

Lucy ventured to guess that Roland knew a brush-off when he encountered one. As a successful doctor, he certainly knew the value of his time. He was most likely an experienced practitioner of the very tactics he deplored in Chief Crowley.

"He's just a small-town cop," said Lucy. "The state police are probably in charge of the investigation."

"I don't care who's in charge. I want some answers. Somebody's gonna have to pay for this," he asserted, slamming his fist on the table and making the crumbs on his plate jump.

"This must be absolutely horrible for you," sympathized Lucy.

"Horrible doesn't begin to describe it." He shook his head. "And it couldn't have come at a worse time. My nomination for the Danforth prize was announced last week, you know."

"I didn't know. Congratulations." She paused. "I'm not familiar with the Danforth. What's it for?"

"The medical society's most prestigious award. It's between me and Feldman, the gastroenterologist. This won't do me much good, I can tell you. The society are a pretty conservative group. They simply will not tolerate the least whiff of scandal."

"How could they hold something as tragic as this against you? I should think you'll get a huge sympathy vote. After all, none of this was your fault."

"You're absolutely right about that. Monica was so stubborn. She always had to have her own way. She wouldn't listen to me. Oh, no! If this was anybody's fault, it was hers."

"Her fault?" Lucy was puzzled. The conversation seemed to have taken a strange turn. Perhaps Roland wasn't quite as distraught as she had first thought.

"She took one look and went running off—wouldn't even wait

for an explanation. That would have required rationality, something Monica didn't have a great deal of."

"She was upset about something?"

"You could say that. What the hell? Everybody has fights, right? We'd been married for a long time. Thirty years."

"That is a long time," agreed Lucy.

"Hey, murder only gets you twenty, twenty-five years in this state, right?" It was an old joke, one he told automatically.

"I guess," said Lucy, trying not to be judgmental. Grief took everyone differently, she reminded herself.

"I gotta get going. Hey, I almost forgot. I stopped by to give you this," he said, rising and shoving the package across the table. "It's a scrapbook Monica kept during the renovation."

"Really?" Lucy was delighted, and deeply moved. "How thoughtful of you to think of us. We'll treasure it always."

"What was I gonna do with it?" he said, as she opened the door for him. "Right now, the fewer reminders I've got to deal with, the better."

CHAPTER NINE

Later that evening, supper over, Lucy gave the kitchen counter one last wipe with the sponge and tossed it into the sink. For the first time since she'd come home from the hospital with Zoe, the kitchen was neat and tidy. The sink was empty of dirty dishes. The counter was clear of clutter. The stove top gleamed. Two dozen Halloween cupcakes, complete with orange icing and candy corn decorations, sat on the kitchen table, ready to be packed in a plastic container and hidden on the top shelf of the pantry.

It was the same with every baby, she thought smugly. The first weeks were always chaotic, the baby's needs came first and everything else was pushed aside. Bit by bit, however, order and routine returned and things fell into place.

The one thing Lucy had worried about most hadn't happened. She had feared that the other children would be resentful of the baby. To her surprise, however, they had taken the new arrival in stride. Toby and Elizabeth were too busy with their friends and school work to be jealous, and Sara was enjoying her new role of big sister. She had even taken photos of the baby to school for show and tell.

All in all, Lucy thought things had turned out better than she had expected. Refusing to think of the unmade beds upstairs, or the piles of dirty laundry in the basement, she congratulated herself for managing so well. Bill was out at his first historical society meeting, Sara was minding Zoe in the family room while she watched TV, Toby and Elizabeth were doing homework at the dining-room table. Deciding she deserved a reward, Lucy pulled a chocolate bar out of the secret stash she kept in the freezer and dialed Sue's number.

"Hello," said Sue.

"Mmmph," responded Lucy. She was working on a rather large chunk of frozen chocolate.

"You'll never lose those extra baby pounds if you don't stop stuffing your face all the time," scolded Sue.

"I was treating myself. After all, I did work out this afternoon," said Lucy, defending herself. "So how's the party coming along?"

"Not bad. Pam Stillings is going to make her famous black punch and she's going to freeze gummi worms in an ice ring."

"Sounds delicious."

"The art classes at the high school are carving pumpkins and making decorations. The Junior Woman's Club is organizing games, and the football boosters are lending us their popcorn machine. The Rotary are handling the apple bobbing—apparently Andy Brown, the guy who owns Farmer Brown's fruit stand, is one of their members. It's all coming together. This Saturday the Scouts and the cheerleaders and anybody else who wants to help are cleaning out the mansion. Can you come, and bring Bill with his hammer, in case there are any loose boards or anything?"

"Sure. What time?"

"Ten?"

"That's good. Sounds like you're really working hard on this."

"Mostly phone calls. I'm delegating. Everybody seems eager to help. Nobody's turned me down. In fact, people have started calling me and offering to help."

"That's great. You'll never guess who paid me a surprise visit."

"Monica's husband?"

"How'd you know?"

"I've been on the phone all afternoon," Sue explained. "I heard he was in town. Pam said he looks terrible. He must be taking this very hard."

"That's what I thought at first, but now I'm not so sure. He seemed more inconvenienced than grief stricken. I got the impression he and Monica hadn't been getting along lately."

"Really?"

"He came right out and told me that he and Monica had a fight, and that's why she was at the Homestead."

"Could be. It's too bad they didn't have a chance to make up."

"Maybe Roland didn't want to make up. Maybe he wanted her out of the way."

"Lucy! How can you think something like that?" Sue was shocked.

"Nine times out of ten it's the husband. He's the one who gave me the idea. He said he'd been married for thirty years and murder only gets you twenty."

"He said that?"

"I think it was a joke he was used to telling at parties—it just came out."

"The poor man probably doesn't know what he's saying. Besides, what about the other fires? Somehow I can't picture him starting all those fires."

"Me, either," agreed Lucy, thinking of the thwarted, repressed individuals the book portrayed as typical arsonists. "Maybe he knew about the fires and planned the murder hoping the police would include it with the others. Kind of a cover-up."

"It must be awful to have a mind like yours—always suspecting the worst."

"Well, my suspicions are not exactly unfounded. When I was buying my gym membership today a funny thing happened. Krissy, you know, the woman who owns the studio, got a phone call. It was from Dr. Mayes, telling her about Monica's death. She didn't look exactly heartbroken."

"Krissy knows Dr. Mayes?"

"Evidently. She said her business partner's wife died in a fire and I asked if it was Monica and she said it was."

"Dr. Mayes is her business partner?"

"That's what she said, but I wouldn't be surprised if he is something more."

"You're disgusting. It's always sex with you, isn't it?"

"Not often enough, according to Bill."

Sue hooted. "Men! You have a baby, and ten minutes later they want to start another one."

"Well, at least Bill has something to keep him occupied. Miss Tilley's got him on the historical commission."

"That's good. About time we got somebody sensible. You know, I think Miss Tilley's losing it. Yesterday I saw her drive right through the stop sign on the corner. She almost hit Franny Small's little blue Dodge!"

"Is everybody all right?"

"I think so. Franny had slowed down to turn the corner. I don't think Miss Tilley saw her. She didn't stop, just went sailing through in that huge car of hers. She came that close—it could have been a real tragedy."

"She knocked over my mailbox the other day. Never even noticed."

"That woman's dangerous. Somebody ought to have a talk with her and get her to give up her license. She shouldn't be driving. It's just a matter of time before someone gets hurt."

"You're right. I'll ask Barney. Maybe she'll listen to him."

"Maybe." Sue was doubtful. "She's awfully stubborn, and determined to be independent. Get this—Karen Baker who works at the bank told me she never cashes her social security checks. The social security people even called to find out if she was dead—Miss T. thought it was a tremendous joke and told Karen all about it."

"Sounds typical. Listen, Sue, I gotta go. Zoe's fussing. I'll call you tomorrow, if I can find a free moment, that is. Between baking cupcakes and working out at the gym I'll probably be very busy."

CHAPTER TEN

Ted Stillings entered the downstairs meeting room at Town Hall and glanced around. The board members were already seated at a long table, which was placed on a slightly raised dais. A small audience had gathered, comprised mainly of applicants and a few Town Hall regulars who never missed a meeting. With a smooth, practiced motion he pulled his reporter's notebook from his back pocket and sat down.

Waiting for the meeting to begin, he tapped his pen lightly against the notebook. Despite the fact that this was his third evening meeting this week, he was looking forward to it. The TCHDC was fast becoming the best show in town. For years, when Miss Tilley and her Gang of Four were in charge, commission meetings were dull and predictable. Although Ted attended faithfully, he didn't have to. He could always predict exactly what the commissioners would say and how they would vote.

When Doug Durning and Jock Mulligan came on board, however, things changed. Stalemated, the commission members vented their frustration by raking one another, and the applicants, over the coals. Their scathing comments made good copy, and circulation always jumped a bit after a TCHDC meeting. Catching his friend Bill Stone's eye, and giving him a big grin, Ted wondered if he knew what he was getting into when he agreed to serve on the board.

"Let's get started," said Miss Tilley, banging her gavel. "This meeting of the Tinker's Cove Historic District Commission is now called to order. Mr. Brown, what can we do for you?"

Andy Brown stood up, hooked his thumbs around the straps of his overalls, and ambled to the front of the room. Considering that Brown was one of the most successful businessmen in town, Ted thought he was carrying the farmer act a bit too far.

"As you prob'ly know, I've got a little farmstand out on Route One. We have a cider press, and we let folks pick their own pumpkins from Farmer Brown's Pumpkin Patch. We've done pretty well, if I do say so myself."

Brown was being deliberately modest, thought Ted. He had discovered gold in those pumpkins, and every year the farmstand grew a bit bigger. This year he had added a haunted hay ride, and the spooky music, groans and screams that emanated from the cornfield at night had prompted several angry letters to the editor.

"We're all familiar with your farmstand," said Miss Tilley.

"Well, what I'd like to do, y'see, is put up one of those portable electric signs, so folks can find the place a mite easier, 'specially at night."

"I find it hard to believe that anyone who is not completely deaf and blind would have the least difficulty finding your establishment," Miss Tilley stated. "Even an electric sign would hardly help such a person. Board, are we ready to vote?"

"Hold yer horses a minute," Brown protested. "My place brings lots of business to this town. Seems to me you could bend the rules, considering how the pumpkin patch extends the tourist season."

"Mr. Brown does have a point," admitted Jock Mulligan, owner of a rather adorable bed and breakfast. "We get quite a few families down from Boston and thereabouts who come especially to visit the pumpkin patch. Grandparents, even, bring the little ones."

"How heartwarming," observed Miss Tilley, with a sneer. "Exactly how large is this sign?"

"It's twelve feet long and eight feet high, and it lights up."

"The sign code clearly forbids lighted signs, and the outside limit is four square feet."

"I know. That's why I'm applying for a variance. This is a portable sign, it will be gone the day after Halloween."

"I don't see any harm in the sign," ventured Doug Durning. "They have something similar for the Blueberry Festival every summer."

"The Blueberry Festival takes place on the other side of town, and it's a fund-raiser for the rescue squad. This is right smack in the center of the historic district," observed Hancock Smith. "You've already got lights strung up all over the place, not to mention that monstrous great pumpkin thing and the sound effects. I agree with Miss Tilley—you couldn't miss the place if you tried."

"Bill, what have you to say?" asked Miss Tilley, giving him an encouraging wink.

"My kids love the pumpkin patch—we go every year," began Bill, giving Brown a nod. "But I have to say the place is pretty eye-catching already. I can't see any need for this additional sign."

"Application denied." Miss Tilley grinned broadly and brought down the gavel. "Next we have Miss Katz."

"It's Kurtz, Tammy Kurtz," corrected an attractive young woman, dressed in a stylish cashmere tunic and pants outfit. "I'm the owner of the Greengage Cafe. As you know, we're located in the rear of the Village Marketplace shopping complex. Under the sign code, we're only allowed one sign, a single board on the large sign that serves the entire complex. Our customers tell us they have trouble finding us, so tonight I'm asking for a variance so we can put up a second sign on the building. I've brought a drawing of the proposed sign with me. As you can see, it's quite attractive and understated."

"That's for us to decide, Miss Kootz," said Miss Tilley, reaching for the sketch with a clawlike hand.

Ted noticed a stiffening of the back under the cashmere, as Tammy stepped forward to hand up the paper.

"This looks very straight forward to me," said Miss Tilley, passing the sketch along. "The sign code clearly specifies that there shall be only one sign for a shopping complex. I will entertain a motion to deny the variance."

She glanced at Hancock Smith, who immediately cleared his voice, obediently preparing to make the motion.

"Not so fast," said Doug Durning. "This lady is trying to run a business, and she's asking us for help to solve a problem. I don't see the harm in one little sign."

"I might point out that if we make an exception for Miss Skootz, we'll have to make an exception for everybody," Miss Tilley huffed. "Why have a sign code at all, if we're not going to enforce it?"

"I've eaten at the Greengage Cafe," offered Jock Mulligan. "I can't remember if I had the Trout en Paupiettes or the Salmon

Timbales on a bed of arugula, it was absolute agony deciding, but I will never forget the Mixed Berry Tiramisu, it was mar-r-rvelous," he said, leaning forward and rolling his eyes. "My congratulations to the chef."

"I don't see what the menu has to do with this matter," said Miss Tilley.

"Oh, but it does. The Greengage Cafe is attracting notice. People come from all over to eat there. It's bringing a very nice class of tourist to our town. Upscale. Just look at the cars in the parking lot. I think we ought to do all we can to help Miss Kurtz succeed."

"It's obvious we have two for and two against," said Miss Tilley. "What does our newest member have to say?"

Bill shifted uncomfortably in his seat as all eyes were focused on him.

"I think that sign at the Village Marketplace complex is confusing. You can't tell what's in there. I'm for granting the variance, and maybe even taking a look at the sign code with an eye to revising it."

"Variance granted, Miss Slutz," said Miss Tilley, banging down the gavel. She looked as if she had a mouthful of tacks, as she flapped the sketch back and forth.

Miss Kurtz smiled sweetly as she stepped forward to retrieve it. "Thank you, Miss Silley," she said. Turning to leave, she gave Ted a wink.

"Next we have Wilpers," said Miss Tilley, frowning as she consulted the agenda. "Anybody named Wilpers here?"

"That's us," said a clean-shaven young man, dressed in a blue oxford cloth shirt and khaki pants. His red face appeared painfully well-scrubbed; the comb tracks were still fresh in his hair. His young wife stood beside him, dressed in a flowered dress with pearl buttons and a lace collar. "We got a notice of violation."

Miss Tilley's eyes widened and she smacked her lips. Scenting blood, Ted thought to himself.

"I believe you're painting your house an unapproved color," she said.

"The house was very run-down when we bought it," said Mrs. Wilpers in a soft voice. "But Buddy and I have worked hard weekends and nights, and it's really starting to come together. It's a Greek Revival style, and we chose a historic color, Woodleigh Sage. I don't know why it's a problem. All the neighbors love it."

"The problem is that your house is in the historic district, and the only approved colors are white, light gray, light yellow and light tan," said Miss Tilley. "You will have to repaint."

Mrs. Wilpers gasped. "But we're almost done. We've been working on this for months."

"You should have checked with us before choosing a color. I've seen it. That house is aqua."

"It's not aqua. It's a historic color. Woodleigh Sage," insisted Mrs. Wilpers.

"Everybody knows that historic houses should be painted white," said Hancock Smith. "That's the way the old-timers did it. That's what looks best."

"Actually," said Bill slowly, "our ancestors used more colors than most people think. White was popular, but green was also used a lot. A much brighter green than you would expect."

"I'm in the real estate business," said Doug. "I know nothing brings property values down faster than allowing people to paint their houses any old color. Next thing you know you've got flamingo pink and the neighborhood's gone to the dogs."

"That's not necessar-r-rily true," said Jock. "If it's used well, color can bring life to a neighborhood."

"This discussion has gone on long enough," said Miss Tilley, sensing rebellion in the ranks. "Who'll give me a motion?"

"I move a finding of fact, that indeed a violation has occurred, and must be rectified within thirty days or the building inspector will issue a fine of fifty dollars per day until said violation is rectified," said Doug Durning.

"All in favor?" Miss Tilley nodded with satisfaction as Durning and Smith raised their hands. "Three to two, the motion passes."

"You have the right to appeal," advised Jock Mulligan. "The regional board is somewhat more . . ." he paused, searching for the right word. "*Au cour-r-ant,*" he finally decided, gave him a chance to show off his French and roll his Rs.

"Next on the agenda," said Miss Tilley, with a bang of her gavel. "We have Mr. Lenk. Good evening, Randy."

Randolph Lenk had not bothered to dress for the occasion, observed Ted. He was still wearing the same oil-stained work clothes he had worn all day. In fact, he had probably worn the same clothes all week. A three-day stubble revealed he hadn't shaved recently, and the lines and creases in his hands were filled with grease. Lenk owned a small, ramshackle Northstar gas station that had been an eyesore on Main Street for years.

"The fellas at the comp'ny say I gotta remodel," began Lenk. "They've drawn up plans—even want a canopy and a convenience maht. They say I gotta do it, or I can't sell their gas anymore."

"I, for one, am glad to hear it," said Doug Durning. "It's long overdue. That place of yours is an embarrassment to the town. Damned valuable property, too. Are those plans you've got there? Let's see 'em."

Lenk shuffled forward and handed up a roll of papers. Durning took them and eagerly began unrolling them, distributing them to the other board members.

"My, my, my," said Jock Mulligan, clucking his tongue.

"It looks like a space ship!" Miss Tilley shrieked.

"There does appear to be an awful lot of plastic and glass," said Hancock Smith, shaking his head. "And that sign. It could be seen for miles."

"That's the idea," agreed Lenk. "Cut down a few of these trees, and folks 'll be able to see it from the Interstate."

"You're planning to cut trees?" Miss Tilley was aghast.

"You know," said Bill, "there's a new appreciation among preservationists for vernacular architecture. It may well be that Mr. Lenk's existing gas station is worth saving. I'd be very surprised if it wasn't a good example of roadside construction from the early Age of the Automobile."

Miss Tilley's eyes widened and she gave Hancock a wry smile. She was beginning to suspect that Bill's appointment might not work out the way she had hoped.

"Since this is such a large project, and it affects so many people, I think we really ought to hold a public hearing," Miss Tilley said. "As proposed this will really change the appearance of the whole town. Especially if trees are cut."

"Are you saying I can't cut trees on my own prop'ty?" Lenk was ready to defend his rights as a landowner.

"We're not saying anything, Mr. Lenk," observed Hancock Smith. "What Miss Tilley has suggested, very wisely, I might add, is that the entire matter be discussed in a public forum. That way, all the interested parties can be heard."

"Who's interested? It's my land. I can do whatever I want." Lenk was beginning to get agitated.

"Your land is in the historic district," explained Doug Durning. "Special rules apply."

"I've got rights," insisted Lenk, raising his voice. "I'm payin' taxes on that land. What happened to democracy?"

"Mr. Lenk," began Jock Mulligan. "Let me assure you that America is indeed, still a democracy. What we must do here, is weigh the rights of the individual against the r-r-rights of the community. Your neighbors also pay taxes, and they have an interest in the appearance of their town. Do you understand?"

"Can I tell Northstar to go ahead, or what? 'Cause if you say no, you're all gonna be sorry. Real sorry." Lenk was at the end of his rope; he was bouncing nervously on the balls of his feet, and rhythmically clenching his hands.

"Nothing will be decided tonight," said Miss Tilley, in the voice that had maintained silence in the Broadbrooks Free Library for more than thirty-five years. "We'll schedule a hearing for next week. Is the board agreed?" Miss Tilley received nods of assent from the other members. "We'll see you next week, Mr. Lenk. Bring whomever you want. Lawyers, company representatives, plans— we'll go over everything. Understood?"

Lenk nodded.

"A word to the wise," she said, leaning forward and waving a gnarled finger at him. "Don't make any changes to that property until you have a certificate of appropriateness from this board. I'm warning you. This board takes violations very seriously."

From the expression on Lenk's face as he headed for the door, Ted was pretty sure the commission was going to have one hell of a fight on its hands.

"Anything else? If not, meeting adjourned," Miss Tilley decreed without calling for a vote. "Oh, Bill, do you have a minute? I have a few thoughts I'd like to share with you."

Poor Bill, thought Ted, standing and slipping his notebook into his pocket. He looked as if he had been caught stuffing overdue books into the Book Return slot. Even though Miss Tilley could no longer charge overdue book fines, she would undoubtedly find some way to make him pay for his insubordination.

CHAPTER ELEVEN

"Did you tape *Seinfeld?*" Bill asked at breakfast the next morning.

Lucy put down the piece of toast she was about to bite and shook her head. "I forgot."

"How could you forget?" demanded Bill.

"Well . . ." said Lucy. "The evening started out peacefully enough but pretty soon the baby began fussing and then Toby couldn't find his gym shoes and Elizabeth needed help finding out why Connecticut is called the Nutmeg State and somehow it was too late and the show was over when I remembered. I'm sorry."

"I only asked you to do one simple thing," continued Bill, unwilling to drop the matter.

"It was only a TV show—it will be rerun before you know it. How was the meeting?" Lucy had been asleep when Bill came home.

"I should never have said I'd be on that damn commission." Bill shook his head and sat down with a cup of coffee.

"That bad?"

"Worse. Miss Tilley was not pleased with me. She told me independence of spirit is a fine thing, but not if it has a negative effect on the community. She also said I was a show-off."

"You? You're usually so quiet."

"I voted to let this couple paint their house green. I told them that early houses were often painted in bright colors but they didn't like it. The approved colors are white, off-white, and gray. Maybe yellow, if it's not too bright."

"It's bound to be a little awkward at first. You all have to get used to one another."

"They brought me on because I'm a restoration carpenter, right? I know about this stuff. It's how I make my living. But they don't want to listen to me. They've got some half-assed idea of what historic means, and they don't want to hear anything different. To them, a house is colonial if it's white and has shutters. They don't even care if the shutters are the right size for the windows. As long as it's a shutter, it's okay."

"Maybe you need to compromise a bit, too," said Lucy. "Nobody today wants to spend a lot of money on authentic shutters they'll never use."

"That's my point. They don't care if it's right. They might as well call it the Pseudo-Historic District, the Disney District. I think I'm gonna resign."

"You can't resign after one meeting."

"Why not? Besides it's gonna take a lot more time than I thought. You wouldn't believe the pages and pages of zoning bylaws she gave me. I'm supposed to 'familiarize myself' with them by the next meeting."

"It'll work out. You'll see. They really need you."

"I doubt it."

"Well, at least give it a while longer. You wouldn't let Toby quit Little League last spring, even though he wanted to. What did you tell him. Only quitters are losers?"

"That's the worst thing about being a parent," said Bill, grinning for the first time that morning. "Your words come back to haunt you."

"That's for sure," said Lucy, getting up to fetch Zoe, who was demanding her breakfast. "Was I the one who said another baby would be no trouble at all?"

Later, after Bill had gone to work and the kids had left for school, and Zoe had been bathed and fed and put down for her morning nap, Lucy got out Monica's book and set it on the table.

It was a wire-bound sketch book, which Monica had covered with blue Waverly plaid fabric. Lucy recognized the pattern, Monica had chosen it for the borning room curtains. She ran her fingers over it, and then opened the book.

The first page had several photographs of the house as it was when the Mayes bought it. Overgrown bushes covered the windows, there was a hole in the roof, and the original pine clapboards were covered with crumbling asphalt shingles.

"My heart stopped when I saw it," Monica had written in bold black ink. "Somehow I knew that this house would be mine. It was the house I'd always dreamed of having."

The statement gave Lucy pause; never in her life had she decided something should be hers simply because she wanted it. For her, life was a constant juggle of too little time, too little money, and too much to do.

Turning the pages, Lucy saw photos chronicling every stage

of the restoration process. The plaster was stripped away from the walls, revealing the aged wood lath underneath. The chimney was torn down and rebuilt. The roof was replaced with bright new cedar shingles.

Lucy smiled to see snapshots of Bill and herself. He looked impossibly young. She, pregnant with Toby, was absolutely huge. There were also photos of Monica's teen-aged children, tan in swimsuits, scraping the paint off a door. Their names were obligingly penned in beneath the pictures: Rolly, Mira, and Tiny. Monica, Lucy remembered, had a penchant for nicknames.

Once the house had been made sound and weather tight, Monica had focused her attention on decorating it. There were pictures of furniture found at auctions, paint chips, and fabric scraps. Sketches showed how each room was arranged. Once she had made a decision, recalled Lucy, Monica never changed her mind. She was not one to spend an afternoon rearranging the furniture.

Closing the book, Lucy clutched it to her chest. She leaned back in her chair and stared at the ceiling. She tried to guess how much the restoration had cost, but couldn't even remember how much Bill had charged.

Curious, she climbed upstairs to the little attic room he used for an office. There, under the slanted ceiling, he had set up a drafting table and a couple of file cabinets.

His files, as she discovered when she pulled out a drawer, were neater than she would have expected. She had no trouble at all finding the thick folder for the Hopkins Homestead. Lucy sat down at the desk and pushed aside the big stack of zoning bylaws Bill had left there. She opened the file; right on top was the estimate he had drawn up—labor and materials came to nearly one hundred thousand dollars.

Lucy whistled softly under her breath. She had no idea. And

this was more than ten years ago—it would be a lot more at today's prices. Bill's figures didn't include the cost of the property itself, or what Monica had spent to furnish or decorate the place. Lucy wouldn't have been surprised if Monica's little project—the house she was determined to have—had cost Roland close to a quarter of a million dollars. Lucy even remembered Monica joking about it, she had once said Roland would have to deliver a lot of babies to pay for it.

Thinking back, Lucy couldn't recall even one picture of Roland Mayes in the scrapbook. It was a real old-fashioned marriage, thought Lucy. He made the money, and Monica spent it.

Closing the file to replace it, Lucy's eyes fell on a penciled phone number. Monica had given it to them a few years ago, when she had taken a trip. They had agreed to keep an eye on the Homestead, and if anything happened, they were supposed to call Mira. She was married, now, and lived in a Boston suburb with her husband and baby. Impulsively, Lucy reached for the phone, then hesitated. She certainly didn't want to add to the woman's grief by asking a lot of questions. On the other hand, she rationalized, it wouldn't hurt to let Mira know that others shared her grief.

"Mira? This is Lucy Stone, in Tinker's Cove. I wanted to call and let you know how sorry I am about your mother."

"Lucy, thanks for calling. It's so sweet of you."

"It's the least I could do. I feel absolutely awful about the fire."

"I don't think I've really taken it in yet. I keep expecting Mom to call and ask how I'm feeling." Mira paused. "I'm pregnant again, you know."

"I didn't know," said Lucy, thinking how sad it was that Monica would never see her second grandchild. "When are you due?"

"In about a month."

"And how old is the baby?"

"Freddie's almost two."

"You'll have your hands full." What a shame, thought Lucy, for Mira to lose her mother just when she needed her so much.

"I sure will," said Mira, her voice trembling.

"I don't want to keep you," said Lucy quickly. "I was just wondering when the service will be. I didn't see anything in the paper."

"I know." Mira fell silent. "I'm ashamed to say we haven't planned anything yet. It's all been so sudden. We're still in shock. You'd think something like this would make us all closer but instead it's ripping the family apart."

"Oh, Mira, every family's different. There's no right way to deal with death." Lucy hesitated a moment, then plunged ahead. "I saw your dad yesterday. He came by the house. He seems to be taking it pretty hard."

"Harder than I expected, that's for sure." There was an edge to Mira's voice. Lucy wondered how much Mira knew about her father and Krissy.

"Well, as you said, it was very sudden."

"Very convenient if you ask me." There was no mistaking the anger in Mira's voice. "He'd told Rolly he was thinking of divorcing Mom. There was somebody else."

"Oh, no. Did your mother know?"

"I don't know how she could have missed it. Everybody knew. I used to see his Mercedes and Krissy's Fiero parked side by side all over town." Mira sniffled; Lucy was pretty sure she was crying. Suddenly, Lucy was ashamed of herself. She didn't want to add to Mira's pain.

"I'm sorry, Mira. I shouldn't have called."

"I'm glad you called," sobbed Mira. "I've felt so alone, like I'm the only one who loved her. It really helps to know that you cared about her, too. I'll let you know when we decide on a time for the service."

"Oh, Mira," said Lucy, her voice breaking. "Bill and I both loved her. She was very special to us. If there's anything we can do to help, please let us know." Lucy wiped her eyes and hung up the phone. Suddenly shaky, she sat down at the kitchen table. She crossed her arms across her stomach and hugged herself, waiting for the sick feeling to go away.

This was ridiculous, she thought. Mira had confirmed her suspicions about Dr. Mayes and Krissy. She was right after all. So why did she feel so horrible?

CHAPTER TWELVE

"Oh, Mrs. Stone. Back already?" Krissy looked up from the class schedule she was decorating with little jack-o'-lanterns. "Vicki may have forgotten to mention it, but it's better to wait a day or two between sessions."

"Really?" said Lucy, feigning disappointment. "That's too bad. I was really counting on another workout before the weekend."

"I wouldn't advise it," said Krissy, staring right through her. The dazzling smile was definitely gone, Krissy seemed almost hostile. Lucy wondered why. Was it because Lucy had told her she knew Monica?

"Oh, well, there's something else I wanted to talk to you about." Lucy glanced around the counter area that was open to the public. "Is there someplace a bit more private, like an office, where we could talk?"

"I'm afraid not," said Krissy flatly.

"I suppose you haven't even finished unpacking yet," said Lucy, refusing to be deterred. "Never mind," she said, leaning over the counter and lowering her voice. "A group of us mothers are putting on a Halloween party for the kids. To try and keep them off the streets, you know. We're cleaning up the old Hallett house this weekend. Would you like to help?"

"I'm afraid I couldn't possibly. Allergies."

"Oh, I didn't mean for you to help with the cleaning," said Lucy with a little laugh. "A lot of businesses in town are making donations."

"A donation?" Krissy looked relieved. "Sure. Is twenty-five dollars okay?"

"More than okay. Terrific," said Lucy, accepting the cash. "Thanks so much."

"No problem," said Krissy, dismissing her and turning back to the schedule she was decorating.

"So, what made you decide to open a studio in Tinker's Cove?" Lucy asked, ignoring the cue.

"I was tired of working for other people. I tried giving private lessons, but, well, the customers kind of got on my nerves."

"Like Monica?" Lucy smiled slyly, and leaned forward slightly. She wanted to give Krissy every encouragement to discuss her rival.

"Oh, that's right. You said you knew her." Krissy was wary.

"My husband did some carpentry work for her." Lucy lowered her voice. "Very demanding. A real pain in the you know what."

"Tell me about it," said Krissy, succumbing to temptation. "She had nothing to do all day, she didn't work or anything, but she still had to keep changing appointments. Sometimes ten minutes before she was due I'd get a call. Can we make it tomorrow instead? So inconsiderate. Never occurred to her that my income depended on a full schedule. And my other clients didn't appreciate getting moved all around to accommodate her. But that was the least of it. She was so rude to me. Treated me like I wasn't as good as her. Nobody was, not even her husband. She was really nasty to him. She really didn't understand him."

Some things never change, thought Lucy. "Sounds typical. A lot of summer people are like that. They think the town was created for them. Never occurs to them that we were here first. So how do you like Tinker's Cove?"

"Everybody's so nice. Just folks. And the ladies seem real pleased to have a place of their own to work out."

"You've really made it attractive." Lucy waved an arm, indicating the mauve carpeting and freshly sandblasted brick walls. "Nobody would guess they used to can sardines here. Not a trace of the old smell."

"We have a really good ventilation system," said Krissy. "And you wouldn't believe the amount I spend on air freshener."

"I've heard it's really hard for women to get small business loans. Did you have any trouble?"

"Not really. I have a partner—he invested some of his own money and arranged for me to borrow the rest."

"Oh, that's right. Didn't you say Dr. Mayes is your partner?"

"Did I say that?" At least Krissy had the decency to blush.

"Yes, I think you did. You said your partner's wife had been killed in a fire and I asked if it was Monica and you said . . ."

"I may have," Krissy interrupted, glancing at a couple of women who had just entered. She greeted them and they gave her a wave, proceeding on into the dressing room. "I don't think he wants it widely known. He's kind of a silent partner—really just doing me a favor. He's such a sweet guy."

A real philanthropist, thought Lucy. "He dropped by at my house the other day. He seemed pretty upset."

"Oh, yes," agreed Krissy. "He's devastated. That fire was some shock."

"They say it was arson. Do you have any idea who could have set it?"

"No." Krissy shook her head. "Some maniac, I guess."

"Lots of times it's the owner."

"Dr. Mayes would never do a thing like that. He's a healer, he helps people."

She was partly right, thought Lucy. He was a heel, at any rate. "Just between you and me . . . do you think he'll remarry? He's quite a catch."

"I wouldn't be surprised," said Krissy, giving Lucy a small, conspiratorial smile.

"Listen, I'm really stiffening up since my workout yesterday. Do you think I could use the exercycle?"

"That's probably not a bad idea," said Krissy, happy to oblige her new friend.

As Lucy pedaled she allowed her mind to drift, thinking over her conversation with Krissy. She didn't like to label people, but Krissy seemed like a classic bimbo. She hadn't come right out and admitted she was Dr. Mayes's lover, but she had implied it. And there was no love lost between her and Monica. She certainly stood to benefit from Monica's death. Now Roland was free to marry her. Could she have somehow lured Monica to the Homestead, and set the fire?

Lucy doubted it. Krissy didn't seem like the kind of girl who would handle the dirty work herself. Not if there was a man she could convince to do it for her.

CHAPTER THIRTEEN

The weekend did not start well. Lucy had no sooner poured herself a cup of coffee on Saturday morning when the phone rang. It was Lorna Phipps, Stubby's mother.

"You have simply got to get control of that son of yours," began Mrs. Phipps, in her usual tone of righteous indignation. Since her son, Stubby, had been the class scapegoat since kindergarten, she had plenty of practice.

"What's he done, now, Lorna?" asked Lucy.

"Well, Toby and those friends of his, Eddie Culpepper and Rickie Goodman and Adam Stillings tossed my Stubby's gym shoes up in the air until they caught on the electric power line. I had to call the electric company to get them down."

"I do apologize. I'm sure it wasn't intentional, it must have been an accident."

"Accident, my eye. Of course they did it on purpose. They had no business taking Stubby's sneakers in the first place. They're always teasing and tormenting him."

Lucy knew this was true. Stubby, overweight and with an overprotective mother, was a natural victim. When Lucy had been the boys' Cub Scout den mother her biggest challenge each week had been trying to think of something for the boys to do that was more interesting than picking on Stubby.

It had been an almost impossible task. Stubby seemed to invite abuse. He stood a little bit too close, he asked stupid questions, he picked his nose. That didn't excuse his tormenters, however.

"I'll talk to Toby," promised Lucy, as a horrifying scene right out of *The Lord of the Flies* played in her mind. "They didn't actually take the shoes right off him, did they?"

"No. They were his gym shoes. They offer no support whatsoever. Dear Stubby has flat feet, you know, and has to wear good, sturdy oxfords. So difficult to find nowadays."

"I bet they are," said Lucy, her heart going out to poor Stubby. With a mother who insisted upon dressing him in sensible shoes and a bow tie for school, he didn't stand a chance.

"Perhaps if you let him dress more like the other boys, they wouldn't tease him so much," she ventured.

"How dare you, Lucy Stone! Just because I refuse to let Stubby dress like those young hooligans, your son included, I might add, that's no excuse for them to tease him."

"Of course not," agreed Lucy. "You're absolutely right."

"And you haven't heard the last of this, I can tell you that. All this happened at the school bus stop, and I am going to make sure the principal hears about it. Those boys could lose their bus privileges, you know."

"I know," admitted Lucy, wondering how she was going to find time in her morning schedule to chauffeur Toby to school.

As soon as she had hung up, she yelled up the stairs. "Toby, get down here this instant."

"Sure, Mom, what's up?" From his sheepish expression, it was clear he knew exactly what was up.

"What's all this about Stubby's shoes?"

"We were just playing keep-away and Eddie tossed 'em up and they got stuck on the wire. Kind of a freak accident."

"You boys have got to stop teasing Stubby. It's mean. Why do you do it?"

"I dunno." Toby looked at his feet.

"How would you like it if the boys did it to you?"

"Not much, I guess."

"Well, stop doing it, okay?"

"Okay." He silently observed a moment of penance, then looked up. "Mom, what's for breakfast?"

Lucy poured herself a big glass of orange juice and joined him at the table. As she watched him wolf down a huge bowl of cereal, and then pour himself a second, she wondered if she had been stern enough with him. He didn't seem to be taking this very seriously. What else had he been up to?

She studied her son, thinking that in many ways he was already a stranger to her. Teetering on the brink of adolescence, his face still pudgy and round, she thought of the pending onslaught of hormones that would carry him even further away from her. Had it already started? What did he do when he was out with his buddies? Could they have set the fires? On a dare, maybe. Or carried away on a sudden surge of testosterone? The thought gripped her, filling her with anxiety.

"Mom, are you okay?" asked Toby. "Why are you looking at me like that?"

"Oh, nothing," she said, giving him a hug. "I was just thinking how fast you're growing up. It's kind of scary."

"Oh, Mom," he groaned, wriggling away and heading for the stairs.

It was a few minutes past ten when Lucy loaded the kids into the Subaru for the short drive to the Ezekiel Hallett house. When they arrived, the ramshackle old mansion was already abuzz with activity. The lawn was filled with cars and trucks; it seemed as if the entire town had turned out to help.

"Hi, Lucy. I see you brought the whole crew," said Sue, trotting up to the car and checking her clipboard. "Where's Bill?"

"He's working this morning. He'll be over later. I've got his lunch."

"I knew I could count on you," said Sue with a smile. "Okay, Toby, you can help the boys carry out trash. Girls, find Miss Perry, the high school art teacher—she's in charge of making decorations. Lucy, I know you've got the baby. Could you sweep and keep an eye on the kids?"

"Sure. I even brought my own broom."

"Great. Oops, I see some more new arrivals. Gotta go."

Lucy watched the busy scene for a minute, thinking how nice it was to see people rally for a common cause. Then, she transferred Zoe from the car safety seat to the red corduroy pouch she wore on her chest. Toting her dustpan and broom, she climbed the hill to the mansion.

"Oh, Mrs. Stone, can I see the baby?"

"Sure," said Lucy, pausing so Jennifer Mitchell could stroke Zoe's cheek. Jennifer, now a junior in high school, occasionally baby-sat for the older kids, but so far Lucy had been reluctant to leave Zoe.

"Isn't she adorable? How old is she now?"

"Six weeks," said Lucy.

"Is she heavy? I know a lot of mothers use those carriers—is it comfortable?"

"You get used to it," said Lucy. "Babies love them. They like being close to Mommy."

"Look at those bright eyes," cooed Jennifer. "She's watching everything."

"She'll doze off pretty soon. Listen, Jennifer. Have you done much sitting for babies?"

"Oh, yeah. I worked all last summer as a mother's helper for Mrs. Cunningham. She had twins—Bridget and Brendan. They were premature and had apnea monitors for a while. They needed special formula, too, and were on a high-frequency schedule. Plus the meds, of course."

Lucy was impressed. "I guess you could manage Zoe, then. She's a normal, full-term baby."

"That'd be great. I've missed playing checkers with Sara."

"How about next Thursday? I want to go to that gas station hearing. It shouldn't be too late, but it'll give you a chance to get acquainted with the baby."

"Sounds super," said Jennifer, with a huge smile.

"I'll pick you up around six-thirty?"

"You don't need to do that. I can drive, now," said Jennifer, beaming with pride. "I passed my driver's test on the first try."

"Congratulations," said Lucy, who still remembered bursting into tears when she failed her first attempt. "Have you got a car?"

"I do. I bought it with my baby-sitting money. It's that little red Toyota." She pointed to a tiny Tercel, rather the worse for wear.

"It doesn't look like much, but it runs good. And it goes forever on a tank of gas."

"That's terrific. I'll see you a little before seven on Thursday?"

"You can count on me," said Jennifer, running off to help her friends, who were struggling to carry a mildewed old mattress to the Dumpster.

Lucy's progress up the hill was slow. She kept meeting people who hadn't seen her since Zoe's birth and wanted to peek at the baby. Finally, making her way into the entrance hall, Lucy paused to examine the plans Sue had tacked to the wall. Games would be located in the ballroom, and refreshments in the drawing room and parlor, while the stairs and a few upstairs rooms would be transformed into a "Trail of Terror" by the high school drama club.

"Whaddya think?" asked Sue, materializing beside her with two styrofoam cups of coffee.

"I think it's going to be a great party," said Lucy, accepting a cup.

"I didn't bring you any donuts—Jake's donated them—because I know you're trying to lose those extra baby pounds," reminded Sue.

"Thanks, so much," said Lucy, who was starving and could have eaten half a dozen. She consoled herself by nuzzling the baby's head with her chin.

"I have your best interests at heart," Sue assured her. "Are you sure Bill's coming? I need someone to tighten up the banister—I don't want any accidents."

"I'm absolutely, one hundred percent sure he'll come. I told you, I've got his lunch."

"Pretty clever. And I thought he was a conscientious, helpful sort of guy."

"He is," admitted Lucy. "Not like some men." She took a sip of coffee.

"Are you thinking of anyone in particular?" Sue leaned against the stained plaster, and settled in for a chat. It had been a long morning and she was ready for a break.

"Monica's husband. He *was* having an affair. With Krissy, just like I thought."

"How do you know?" Sue wasn't convinced.

"I called Monica's daughter, Mira. She told me. Then I happened to see Krissy at the gym and asked a few questions. It all adds up to a pretty big motive, if you ask me."

"Lucy, you're taking this stuff too far. If you keep poking around in other people's business you're going to get in trouble. In fact, someone's staring at you in the weirdest way right now."

"Who?" Lucy whirled around and saw Lorna Phipps peering at her from a doorway. She gave her a cheery wave, but Lorna did not return it.

"That's just Stubby's mom—she disapproves of me," said Lucy, with a wave of her hand. "That has nothing to do with this. Don't you see? If he was having an affair, that would be a motive, wouldn't it? Say he wanted to marry Krissy."

"You've never heard of divorce?"

"You've never heard of alimony?" Lucy shot back. "Maybe he wanted to get rid of her and keep his money. Maybe he was afraid Krissy wouldn't be interested in him without his dough."

"It seems pretty risky to me. What if he got caught? Then he wouldn't be able to enjoy Krissy or his money,"

"Well, he's gotten away with it so far. And if it hadn't been for the dog, the body might never have been discovered," Lucy pointed out. "It was almost a perfect murder."

"What about the car?"

"You've got me there," admitted Lucy, running out of answers. "He should have gotten rid of it."

"See. It was an accident. Monica was in the wrong place at the wrong time."

"Maybe," agreed Lucy, draining her coffee and tossing the cup in a convenient trash barrel. "Time to get to work," she said, taking up her broom and beginning to sweep.

"Let me know as soon as Bill comes, okay?" Sue made a note on her clipboard and hurried off.

Buckling down to her job, Lucy soon had a sizable pile of dirt in the middle of the floor. Moving awkwardly because of the baby carrier, she was bending down to sweep it into the dustpan when she was almost knocked off her feet by Toby and Eddie, who were running through the foyer.

"Hey, watch it," she said sharply. "You're gonna hurt somebody."

"That's right, boys. Slow down," roared Barney, clamping his hands on Eddie and Toby's shoulders and stopping them in their tracks. "What's the idea, anyway?"

"We're helping," offered Toby.

"What's that you got there?" demanded Barney.

"It's a walkie-talkie. Rickie got 'em for his birthday."

"Where's Rickie?"

"We're trying to find him and Adam."

"That's how you're helping? You're running all over, chasing your buddies?"

"I guess."

"Gimme that," ordered Barney, taking the toy. "I'll find them. You find Mrs. Finch and she'll tell you how you can help. Okay?"

"Okay," agreed Eddie and Toby.

Barney pushed down the button on the walkie-talkie. "Boys,

this is Officer Culpepper. Get your butts in here this minute and report to Mrs. Finch. Got that?"

A high squeaky voice came through the static. "Got it."

Lucy laughed. "Those boys are driving me crazy. Did you hear about Stubby's shoes?"

"Marge mentioned it." Marge was Barney's wife. "I had a little talk with Eddie."

"I had one with Toby. Do you think it will do any good? Is this thing out of control?"

"I don't think so. Kids tease each other. It's not nice, but it's normal. To tell the truth, Stubby kinda asks for it."

"I know. Somebody ought to tell him how to stick up for himself."

"That's a good idea, Lucy. I think I'll have a little talk with Stubby myself."

"Don't let Lorna catch you. She's determined Stubby won't be a hooligan like our boys."

"I can tell her a thing or two about youthful offenders—real sickos—that'll keep her awake at night."

"That reminds me—any progress on the fires?"

"Well, the fire marshal's office had us bring in anybody with a previous record of arson—arrests, mind you, not convictions. Computer gave us eight or nine names, but it turned out none of them could've set all the fires. The fires were started the same way, according to the state fire marshal, so they're pretty sure it's the work of one person. Could be somebody new, just discovered he likes to play with matches, or could be the fires are a cover-up for some other crime."

"Like murder?"

"Could be murder, could be insurance fraud, could be a nut.

They're looking at everything. The word I've heard is that this case is going to be cracked in the lab."

"What do you mean?"

"They've got solid evidence of some kind—DNA, fibers, I dunno. Nobody's talking. They've really clamped a lid on it."

"Did they question Dr. Mayes? His daughter told me he was having an affair. He might have wanted Monica out of the way."

Barney nodded. "Oh, sure. He was the first one they questioned. Had an ironclad alibi. In surgery or something."

Lucy was disappointed. "Oh. Maybe he hired somebody."

"Maybe. If he did, we've still gotta figure out who it was. We're back at square one."

"I guess so." Lucy sighed. "There was something I wanted to talk to you about, but I can't remember what it is. Darn. I hate it when that happens. They say the short-term memory is the first to go."

"Give me a call when you think of it." He fingered the toy walkie-talkie he had confiscated from Toby. "I think I'll see if I can find Stubby. That boy needs a little man-to-man advice."

Maybe Toby does, too, thought Lucy, deciding to ask Bill to have a little talk with him.

CHAPTER FOURTEEN

Zoe was getting restless inside the baby pouch, so Lucy decided to go back to the car to change her diaper and let her nurse. Lifting the hatchback, she spread out a quilt and laid Zoe on her back. While the baby kicked her arms and legs, Lucy stretched a bit and arched her back.

When Bill slipped his arms around her from behind and nuzzled her neck with his beard, she was momentarily startled.

"What if my husband sees us?" she teased, covering his hands with her own.

"I don't care. I love you more than he does. I have to have you, Lady Dolores."

"Lady Dolores? Can't you do better than that?" teased Lucy. Actually she was delighted by his playfulness. Lately, it seemed he was either installing fire extinguishers or studying those darned zoning bylaws.

"I'm just a poor, humble carpenter," he said with mock humility. "So, what do they want me to do?"

"You better check with Sue. She said something about making sure the stairs are safe."

"Sounds like a good idea. Have you got anything to eat?"

"Sandwiches. PB and J, or tuna?"

"Tuna."

Lucy produced a couple of sandwiches, and a can of soda, and he settled on the way-back to eat while she changed the baby's diaper. That job finished, she sat down beside him to nurse the baby and eat her own lunch.

"Have you ever been unfaithful to me?" asked Lucy.

"What?" sputtered Bill, spraying soda. "What kind of question is that?"

"I just wondered. What makes a man have an affair?"

"Don't ask me. I'm a good boy."

Lucy raised an eyebrow. "Really?"

"Really. It isn't that I haven't been tempted, it's just that I'm usually too tired."

Lucy gave Bill a light punch on the arm. "Thanks a lot."

"Serves you right. Say, don't we have some children? Don't they want lunch?"

"There's a ton of donuts and soda and snacks inside. They probably pigged out as soon as they got here."

"Oh." Bill knew that a steady diet of balanced meals featuring whole grains and plenty of fresh vegetables had left his children extremely susceptible to the attractions of junk food.

"I'm worried about Toby." She looked up at Bill.

"He seems pretty healthy to me, but you could give him vitamins or something."

"Not his diet," said Lucy, smiling and shaking her head. "I'm worried he's going to get into trouble. Serious trouble. Last year he pulled that toilet paper stunt, and Mrs. Phipps told me he and the other boys have been playing cruel tricks on Stubby. I just wonder if he's getting a little wild. And Halloween's the time for it."

"I'll talk to him," said Bill, standing up and stretching. "Well, I guess the faster I get that staircase fixed, the faster I can get home and watch the game."

That will be nice, thought Lucy, watching him trudge up the hill with his heavy toolbox. He'd been so down in the dumps since the fire. Maybe he'd watch with Toby, and they'd drink sodas and eat chips and roar their approval when Notre Dame or Florida State got a touchdown.

Lucy stayed at the car, nursing the baby. Zoe was in no hurry, so Lucy made herself comfortable and reached for another oatmeal cookie.

Looking up at the mansion, Lucy thought how different it looked today. No longer empty and deserted, it seemed to be coming to life once again, thanks to the vitality and energy of the volunteers. Windows were thrown open, voices were heard in the empty rooms, doors slammed as people came and went.

The whole town seemed to have turned out for the cleanup. The ladies from the women's club had arrived early, bringing donated baked goods. "Just something in case people get hungry," said Irma Stout.

All the scouts were there, as well as the high school soccer team and the Alpha club. "The football team had a game," explained Karen Baker, whose oldest son was a defensive end, "or they would have been here, too."

A lot of local businessmen had donated their services; Sue could be very persuasive. Lucy saw the Baxter Electric truck; Larry Baxter must be setting up temporary wiring, she guessed. Harry

Potts had stopped by, too, checking out the best location for his Porta-Potts. Ted Stilling had been busy all morning, snapping pictures and getting quotes.

There must be some way to save this building, thought Lucy. A theater? A restaurant? A bed and breakfast? Maybe the party would attract some entrepreneur, someone who would see the wonderful potential of the old place. Some fresh paint and wallpaper could do wonders.

"Enjoy Victorian elegance at the Hallett House," thought Lucy, picturing a tasteful magazine advertisement, complete with a pen and ink sketch of the Italianate tower. She looked up to the roof, where a flight of curving steps round the tower led to an octagonal platform, where eight pillars supported a roof topped with eight decorative wooden urns.

"Bats in the belfry," was probably more like it, she thought, taking a closer look. A few minutes later, her attention was drawn to the arrival of the fire chief when he pulled up in his bright red sedan. Rearranging her clothes and strapping the baby pouch back in place, Lucy hurried up the hill to hear the results of his inspection.

Entering the hallway once again, she joined the group of anxious volunteers. "He better pass it," whispered Karen Baker. "I hope I didn't get this backache for nothing."

"Yeah," agreed Lucy. "It would be a shame if we couldn't have the party after everyone did so much work."

They all watched as Chief Pulaski came down the stairs. There was a hush as the volunteers waited for his announcement.

"I don't have any problem issuing a temporary occupancy permit," he said, "for one night only—October thirty-one."

The group joined in a collective sigh of relief.

"But," he added, raising a cautionary finger, "there will be absolutely no open flames—no candles, no jack-o'-lanterns, nothing like that. I'm satisfied with the temporary wiring—so let's use it. The last thing we need is another tragedy." Everyone nodded agreement.

"That said, looks like it's gonna be a great party." He signed the certificate with a flourish, and presented it to Sue.

"Happy Halloween, everybody!" she exclaimed, waving it high above her head in triumph. The mothers and fathers, the high school kids, the scouts all smiled and cheered and congratulated one another.

"Party on, dudes!" shouted Rickie Goodman, and everybody laughed, even Stubby Phipps. Stubby, Lucy couldn't help noticing, had abandoned his bow tie, and was clutching a walkie-talkie. Not a toy like Rickie's; this was an official police issue hand radio. It looked like Barney had made his first move in the campaign to make Stubby socially acceptable.

Lucy rounded up the kids and herded them toward the car, thinking of the chores that awaited her at home.

"Girls, how would you like to bake some cupcakes this afternoon?" she asked, as she made sure everyone was safely strapped in.

"Yeah," said Sara, her eyes brightening at the thought of licking the icing bowl.

"Do we have to?" protested Elizabeth.

Lord, give me strength, prayed Lucy silently, as she started the engine. Backing the car around, she glanced up at the Hallett house one more time. If that psychology book was right, she thought, the towering mansion would present an irresistible temptation to a pyromaniac. Steering the car down the dusty driveway, she couldn't help wondering if the old house would still be standing for the party next weekend.

CHAPTER FIFTEEN

Lucy was juggling the baby and a cup of coffee on Monday morning when the phone rang and Bill answered upstairs. He was grinning like the proverbial Cheshire cat when he appeared in the kitchen a few minutes later.

"We won the lottery?" she asked.

"Not quite—but almost. That was Shelburne Village."

"No." Lucy's tone was suitably reverent; Shelburne Village was the premier restoration project in New England, maybe the entire country.

"Yeah. That was them. They saw my letter in *Architectural Heritage* magazine, and they want me to take a look at a door. They want to know if it's as old as they think it is."

"Wow. That's great. What an honor."

"They want me to come today. It's awfully short notice and I'll have to spend the night. Can you manage all alone?"

"Sure. I'm a big girl."

"Three kids and a baby—it's an awful lot."

"I'll manage just fine," insisted Lucy. She would never have admitted it, but she secretly enjoyed Bill's rare absences. It was a chance to relax the rules a bit—instead of cooking meat and potatoes for supper she was already planning to mix up big bowls of macaroni and cheese for the kids to eat in front of the TV. After the hurly-burly of the weekend she was looking forward to having the house, and the baby, to herself.

So, after the kids left for school, and Bill finally finished packing and left for his trip to Vermont, and Zoe settled down for her morning nap, Lucy fixed herself a cup of decaf mocha and tackled the bills. If only the kids would turn off the lights once in a while, she thought, writing out a check for $87.73 for the electric company. The phone bill wasn't too bad, only $37.16 including the weekly long-distance chat with her mother in New York. The heat bill, $154.65 on something mistakenly called the budget plan, sent her scurrying to turn down the thermostat. If they wore sweaters and drank hot liquids, sixty-two degrees would be plenty warm enough.

Preparing to write out a $390 check for homeowner's insurance, thankful that it came only once a year, she noticed the house was valued at $165,000. That was a lot of money, she thought.

Insurance fraud, she remembered Barney saying, was a possible motive for the fires. Certainly not for the barn, or the powder house. Possibly for the theater, though Lucy doubted the very respectable members of the board of trustees at Winchester College would stoop to such a thing. That left the Homestead.

It must have been insured for a pretty penny, she guessed. If replacement value was the guide used by insurance companies, it would certainly be very expensive to accurately reconstruct an antique house like the Homestead.

She knew it represented a sizable investment on the part of Dr. Mayes, something in the neighborhood of a quarter million dollars. That was a lot of money, especially if you weren't getting any return on it. Lucy knew that Dr. Mayes had little interest in the house, it had been Monica's project from the start. She hadn't even referred to it as "theirs" remembered Lucy, it was always "her" house.

Suddenly Dr. Mayes seemed to have plenty of reasons to burn down the house. Not only would he get rid of Monica, and conveniently dispose of her body at the same time, but he would also get back the money he had invested in the house. Add to that the fact that he wouldn't be faced with a messy and expensive divorce, and it seemed more than likely that Dr. Mayes was responsible for the fire.

That meant the fire was premeditated; he had to have carefully planned the whole thing. Maybe the three earlier fires had given him the idea. What an opportunity—investigators would assume the Homestead fire was just another arson, not a murder. All he had to do was lure Monica to the Homestead. Then, once she was there, it would be simple enough to set the fire. End of Monica.

Lucy shivered, suddenly chilly, and wrapped her arms across her chest. He had lived with Monica for thirty odd years. They had raised a family, they had shared the same bathroom, eaten meals together, slept side by side. And then at some point, perhaps when she was leafing through a magazine or sipping her morning cup of coffee, he had decided to kill her.

Lucy reached for the phone and dialed the police station. She asked for Officer Culpepper and was surprised when she was connected; usually she had to leave a message and wait for him to call back.

"Barney, why aren't you out keeping the streets of Tinker's Cove safe for honest citizens?"

"Paperwork," he grumbled.

"Listen, Barney, I've got an idea about the fires."

"I'm listening."

"Well, it just occurred to me that Dr. Mayes had an awful lot of reasons to burn down the Homestead. One, he could get rid of his wife without paying alimony; two, he would be free to do whatever he wants with Krissy; three, he would get insurance money for the Homestead . . ."

"Who's Krissy?"

"Don't you know? She opened that new fitness studio in town—she's the other woman in Dr. Mayes's life, and he's part-owner of the studio."

"Where'd you hear this?" asked Barney.

"You mean you didn't know?"

"Of course we know," said Barney, defending the department. "What I asked is how did you find all this out?"

"I've heard things here and there."

"Lucy, you better mind your own business. I'd hate to see you end up like Mrs. Mayes."

"Barney, you're just trying to scare me. I'm not going to end up like Monica if you guys do your job and arrest Dr. Mayes."

"It's not that simple." Lucy heard Barney sigh.

"How much more do you need? He's got motives on top of motives!"

"That's not enough. Just 'cause he's got a motive doesn't mean he murdered her. Lots of people have got motives—all sorts of motives. That doesn't make them criminals."

"Oh."

"And besides, there are the other fires. The modus was the same. This is basically an arson case."

"Maybe he set all the fires, to cover up the murder," suggested Lucy.

"Lucy, I gotta go," said Barney, running out of patience. "And remember what I said. This is one case you should leave to the professionals."

"Okay, okay," said Lucy, tired of the same old refrain. "Bye now."

As she replaced the receiver Lucy wondered if Dr. Mayes had set all the fires. He was a surgeon, a methodical man. One fire resulting in a death would have been considered murder. A rash of fires, on the other hand, would make it seem as if poor Monica was simply in the wrong place at the wrong time. But could he have done it? Barney had said something about an alibi—he was supposed to be in surgery or something.

What about the other fires? She remembered seeing him at the Fourth of July parade, wondering what had brought him to Tinker's Cove. While Monica always attended, she had usually come with a group of houseguests, Lucy had never seen Dr. Mayes with them. The movie theater had burned that weekend, on July 5. Perhaps that was what brought him to town.

And the second fire, on August 28? Could he have set that one, too? Checking the calendar, Lucy saw that August 28 was a Friday. Was he in his office, she wondered, or was he skulking around Bumps River Road, setting a fire in the old barn?

Grabbing the phone, she called information and got his number. She dialed, then waited for his receptionist to answer.

"Dr. Mayes office."

"This is Gloria at Blue Cross/Blue Shield. I need to verify a patient claim for a D and C supposedly performed by Dr. Mayes on August 28."

"Patient's name, please."

"Kenmore, Joyce," improvised Lucy, happening to spot the brand name on the refrigerator. "Birthdate, June 6, 1963. Social security number . . ."

"That won't be necessary. I'll just check the book." After a pause, she continued. "There must be some mistake. The office was closed that day. I checked our files, too. We have no patient by that name."

"I suspected as much. I knew there was something funny about this one. Thank you for your cooperation. Fraudulent claims cost us all money."

"You're welcome," replied the receptionist. Something in her voice made Lucy wonder if she'd gone a bit over the top. It was so hard to get these impersonations just right.

Encouraged by her discovery, Lucy checked the calendar. September 26, the day the powder house burned, was also a Friday. But how could she find out if Dr. Mayes had an alibi? She could hardly call the office again.

Hearing Zoe fussing upstairs, Lucy reluctantly abandoned playing detective. Besides, she realized, as she climbed the stairs, Dr. Mayes would hardly shut his practice so he could set fires. Most likely he hired a professional. Much less risky. Especially when you considered how the Medical Society deplored scandal.

Back to the drawing board, thought Lucy, settling down in the recliner to nurse Zoe. Where did I leave off, she asked herself, opening up the psychology book and propping it on Zoe's hip.

"Sexual malfunction is almost always associated with the development of the arsonous personality," she read. "Impotence, in particular, often plays a contributing role."

Somehow, she thought with a sigh, that just didn't sound like Dr. Mayes.

CHAPTER SIXTEEN

After lunch, Lucy had planned to take her aerobics class, but first she stopped by at Doug Durning's real estate office on Main Street. She had promised to pick up some information about the upcoming gas station hearing for Bill. Fortunately, there was an empty parking spot right in front.

As Lucy hurried up the front walk, carrying Zoe in her arms, she noticed how similar this building was to the Hathorn-Pye house. Another big, four-square Georgian with a huge center chimney. Opening the front door, however, she was momentarily taken aback. Instead of the big center hallway she had expected, she found herself in a cramped entry, confronted with three doors.

Which one led to the office? Opening the middle one, she found herself looking at a jumble of old office equipment. The faintest whiff of a pungent scent reminded her momentarily of starchy plaid dresses with white collars and her fingers wrapped clumsily around a big yellow pencil.

Closing that door, she opened the one to the left. This was obviously Durning's office, but no one was there. Checking her watch she saw it wasn't quite eleven. When she had called, asking on Bill's behalf if he had any TCHDC minutes or records on Lenk's gas station, he had told her to come by around eleven.

Deciding he would probably be along soon, Lucy went back outside. It was a sunny, crisp fall day, too nice to be inside. Lucy set Zoe back in her safety seat and leaned against the car, looking up and down Main Street. It was the sort of day New England was famous for. The sky was bright blue, the leaves on the maple trees lining the street were bright yellow. The ground was covered with them. Lucy gave a kick, sending up a small shower of rustling gold.

Regarding the stately old homes that sat well back from the street, surrounded by generous yards, Lucy appreciated the value of the commission. Tinker's Cove was a handsome town, thanks in large part to the fine homes built by merchants and sea captains in the last century. Prosperous, and proud of it, they spent their fortunes building large, stately houses.

The age of sail hadn't lasted, of course, and the sea captains eventually fell on hard times, taking the rest of the town down with them. There wasn't any money to add on to the houses, or change them, so they stayed the way they were. A few had been cut up into apartments or rooming houses, but from the outside the street looked much as it had looked a hundred years ago. Although the road was now lined with parked cars, there were still a few mounting blocks and hitching posts, Lucy noticed. Remnants from another age.

She liked that. In New England, people respected the past and were slow to change. She'd visited relatives in the sun belt and been shocked at the raw, utilitarian ugliness of the buildings. The buildings were low and squat, with flat roofs. There were no lofty steeples, no pitched roofs angled against the blue sky. Without the garish, plastic signs you couldn't tell a store from a church or a house. There was no history; everything was new.

Thanks to the recent recession, of course, there hadn't been much new development in Tinker's Cove. Now that the region once again seemed headed for economic recovery, some people claimed the commission stifled initiative and new development. People like Randolph Lenk, for instance.

"Hi, Lucy. Sorry I'm late, I got held up at town hall." Doug was a bit out of breath, as if he'd been hurrying.

He was a good-looking man, not too tall, a touch of gray at the temples. There was something a bit battered, a bit world-weary about him, that Lucy found appealing. She gave him a big smile.

"No problem. I've just been enjoying this beautiful day."

"Come on in and I'll see what I've got for you. You know, Lucy, Bill is a real addition to the commission. He knows his stuff, but he's not fossilized like the others. He knows what it's like to try to run a business and pay the bills."

"He sure does," said Lucy with a smile. "I just have to get the baby, okay?"

Toting the heavy, plastic seat, Lucy followed Doug into the rather bare reception area. A deacon's bench sat under one window, a couple of captain's chairs were pulled up to a desk.

"Sally's only part-time," he said, waving his hand at the empty desk. "I think she keeps the commission stuff in here." He opened a file drawer and began searching. "Hmm, this may take a minute or two. Go on in and sit down in my office—the chairs there are more comfortable."

Still carrying the sleeping Zoe, Lucy went into Doug's office and sat down in an upholstered wing chair. She tried to imagine what purpose this room must have served when the house was built and failed; it seemed too small to have been a parlor or dining room, too large to be a pantry.

Spotting a framed plan, she got up to examine it, and all was made clear. The old house had been completely remodeled inside and the original four rooms and a hall had been transformed into three office suites. The plan was surrounded by a display of photographs, and Lucy was intrigued.

There was Doug shaking hands with Larry Bird, there was a signed photo of hockey great turned businessman Bobby Orr, and a group photo that included Doug, George and Barbara Bush, and five or six others. Leaning closer, Lucy tried to identify the people in the other photos. Except for one rather notorious grouping, a savings and loan president now in jail along with a former state representative currently under indictment, she didn't recognize anyone.

"Here you are, Lucy. She had it filed under T, I can't imagine why."

"Thanks. Bill will really appreciate having some background information. I know he felt a bit at sea at the last meeting."

"It takes awhile to get up to speed."

"I'm sure. This is a wonderful collection of photos." Lucy couldn't resist asking, "How did you happen to meet Larry Bird? What's he like?"

"Real nice. I actually had dinner with him." Doug was on the verge of boasting, but caught himself. "Me and a lot of other people. It was a business thing—a long time ago." He shrugged. "Seems like another life—the fabulous eighties. Those were the days. You could sell anything, for any price. Everybody had money to burn. Not anymore."

"Never, for me," admitted Lucy. "Seems like I've always been pinching pennies. That reminds me. I'm supposed to ask if you could make a donation to the Halloween Party."

"Oh, sure," said Doug, promptly sitting down at his desk and opening a massive checkbook. "That's a great idea, doing something for the kids at Halloween. Keep 'em out of trouble," he said, writing out a check and handing it over.

"Thanks," said Lucy, stuffing the check in her pocket. "I hate asking for money."

"Think nothing of it. It's for a good cause."

"Well, thanks again, for everything. I'll see you at the hearing."

Once again, Lucy picked up the heavy baby seat and lugged it out to the car. Why, she wondered, did Zoe insist on sleeping when it was least convenient? Later, when they got back home and Lucy had dishes to wash and rugs to vacuum and cupcakes to bake, she would be wide awake and demanding attention.

Lucy strapped the car seat in place, and slid under the wheel. Remembering the check in her pocket, she pulled it out and looked at it. Ten dollars. She shook her head. She was going to spend more than that in cupcake mix. What was all that about worthy causes? she wondered, as she turned the ignition. Of course, she admitted with a shrug, with these Yankees you could never tell if they didn't have any money, or just didn't want to spend it.

CHAPTER SEVENTEEN

When Lucy arrived at the Body Shop she discovered she only had a few minutes before her one-thirty class. She quickly dropped Zoe at the child care center and hurried into the locker room to change. Then, taking a place at the back of the room she threw herself into the lesson. As she followed Vicki's instructions, amplified over the thumping beat of a rock song, she imagined the fat melting and slipping off her body, revealing firm, shapely muscles beneath. She lifted her legs and raised her arms, ignoring the aching, burning pain and concentrating on the firm, slim body she was determined to have.

When the class was over she felt a bit light-headed and wobbly so she headed for the juice machine. Sitting on a bench, she sipped a raspberry-kiwi concoction and waited for the sugar to take effect.

"Oh, good," said Vicki, sitting beside her and taking a long drink from a bottle of spring water. "I thought you looked a bit pale. I was going to suggest you have some juice or something."

"How do you do this all day long?" Lucy asked.

"You get used to it," said Vicki, shrugging a smooth bronze shoulder. "So, how do you like the class?"

"Fine, I guess. How long does it take before you notice a difference in your body?"

"After about six weeks you'll begin to see some changes."

"That long?" Lucy was disappointed.

"It takes time—think how long it took for you to get out of shape."

"Getting out of shape was a lot easier than getting back in," said Lucy. "Do you like working here?"

"It's great. I knew Krissy from Boston and I was real excited when she asked me to come up here. I was sick of the city—high rents, dirt, the crowds on the T, the homeless people lying on the sidewalks. Too depressing. Here, everything's clean and pretty."

"Wait till winter," warned Lucy. "There isn't much to do."

"That won't bother me," said Vicki, with a toss of her ponytail. "I'll just curl up by the fire with a good book."

"Have you known Krissy for long?" inquired Lucy.

"We worked at some of the same places, you know. The fitness world is kind of small—you keep running into the same people. But I didn't really know her well until I came here. We worked together all summer, getting this place ready."

"You did?" Lucy was interested. It seemed Krissy had been in Tinker's Cove longer than she thought.

"Yeah. We rented a floor scraper and we nailed up sheetrock and painted it. Krissy even did the electrical wiring."

"You're kidding." Lucy was amazed. Apparently Krissy wasn't quite the dumb blonde she had assumed.

"No, it's true. She knows all about this stuff. She helped her father remodel their house when she was a kid. I just did what she told me but it came out pretty good, don't you think?"

"It really did," agreed Lucy. "But isn't wiring kind of tricky? I mean, what if she made a mistake and crossed some circuits or something?"

"Then we'd have a big problem, I guess. But everything seems to be working just fine. Sound system, ventilation, lights, you name it. Listen, I gotta go. My body sculpting class is waiting for me." She paused for emphasis. "Those girls are serious, believe me."

Lucy glanced at the clock, shocked to see how late it was. She had better get moving, she decided, tossing her juice can in the recycling bin next to the machine. She was supposed to pick up the kids at school and meet Sue for a trip to Andy Brown's pumpkin patch. She quickly showered, passed the blow dryer over her hair, threw on her clothes, and headed for the nursery where she found Zoe fussing in a crib.

"I tried everything I could think of," apologized the attendant. Lucy knew from the sign on the door that her name was Peggy and she was a nursing student at the community college. "I finally put her down, hoping she'd go to sleep."

"That's okay," said Lucy, "I think she's working on a tooth or something." She picked up Zoe and tucked her under her chin for a cuddle. Zoe gave a little snort, sighed, and promptly went to sleep.

"I guess that explains it. She just wanted her mommy," said Peggy.

"It's wonderful to be needed," Lucy said, hurrying off. She was halfway down the hallway, past the office, when she heard Krissy's voice.

"I can't believe this," Krissy sobbed. There was a pause. When she spoke again, she sounded angry. "Not after all I've done for you. Doesn't that mean anything to you?"

Lucy stepped closer, straining to hear. Then Zoe stirred against her chest and began to fuss. "Shhh," she whispered, rubbing her chin against Zoe's head.

Zoe was not about to be soothed. She took a deep breath, winding up for a full-blown cry.

Reluctantly, Lucy pulled herself away from the doorway and hurried down the hall. "It's okay," she murmured, patting the baby's back and gently bouncing her. She pushed open the door and crossed the parking lot toward her car.

At first she didn't notice anything wrong. It was only when she reached for the door handle that she saw the damage.

A long, jagged line of black paint had been sprayed along the side of her car.

CHAPTER EIGHTEEN

"I guess Halloween came early this year," said Sue, eyeing the damage a few minutes later. She licked a finger and rubbed the black streak. "Lucky for you, it seems to be water soluble."

"I'll try the car wash. Hop in, I'm running late. The kids got out of school five minutes ago."

Sue hopped into the car next to Lucy, and fastened her seat belt. "So, how's the investigation going?"

Lucy didn't need much encouragement and started right in. "I was pretty convinced it was Dr. Mayes—after all, ninety percent of the time it's the husband. But now I'm beginning to think Krissy might have done it. It turns out she's very handy. Vicki told me all about how she spent the summer wiring the gym."

"You think Krissy set the fires?" Sue was intrigued.

"She was here, and she knows all about electricity. And once she got Monica out of the way she'd have Dr. Mayes all to herself.

But I'm not convinced. I've been reading this psychology book and it says arson is predominantly a male crime."

"Most crimes are," said Sue. "But don't forget, this is an equal opportunity society. Girls can do anything boys can. Personally, I wouldn't put anything past her. She's entirely too . . ." Sue paused, looking for the right word. "Fit."

"By the way, I haven't seen you at the gym," said Lucy, pulling up in front of the school.

"I haven't had time."

"Excuses, excuses," said Lucy, shaking her head. "Hop in kids—Toby, you'll have to get in the wayback."

"You were late, Mom," said Elizabeth, climbing into the back seat. "We had to wait forever."

"Who painted the car?" asked Sara.

"Bad boys, most likely," said Lucy, catching Toby's eye in the rearview mirror. "I hope none of you would ever do such a thing."

"Mom, wash it off! It's bad enough I have to ride around in this beat-up old Subaru . . . what if somebody sees me?" Elizabeth was acutely self-conscious.

"Somebody like Matt Price?" teased Toby.

"No-o-o." Elizabeth's voice was scornful. "I don't care if Matt Price sees me."

"Who, then? Stubby Phipps? He told me he likes you."

"Stubby is disgusting. Almost as disgusting as you."

"Stop bickering, or we won't go to the pumpkin patch," warned Lucy. "We'll go straight home."

"Mom, are we almost there?" asked Toby. "It's not very comfortable back here."

"Almost," answered Lucy. "It's just down the road a little bit."

Even though the farmstand was on the outskirts of town, it

was still in the historic district. Wary of commercialization, the town had voted to extend the district along Main Street to the town boundary.

"Can we go on the haunted hayride?" asked Elizabeth.

"That's at night. We're only here to get a pumpkin. A perfect pumpkin."

"What's a perfeck pumpkin?" asked Sara.

"We'll know when we see it," said Lucy, spotting a sign for Farmer Brown's Pumpkin Patch. "I think we're getting close."

Coming around a bend, Lucy couldn't help gasping as the full glory of Farmer Brown's was revealed to her. The farmstand itself was an old barn, painted the TCHDC-approved shade of yellow, but outlined with strings of orange lights. Constrained by the stringent sign code, Andy Brown had not hesitated to improvise. He had constructed a platform above the barn entrance, and arranged shocks of corn, bales of hay, and numerous harvest figures made from stuffed overalls with pumpkin heads. To the left of the barn another platform had been erected, this was a shrine to the 775-pound winner of Farmer Brown's annual contest for the biggest pumpkin.

Acres and acres of pumpkins, still clinging to their withered vines, surrounded the farmstand, along with acres and acres of parking. Hay wagons, pulled by small red tractors ferried customers from their cars and out to the farther reaches of the pumpkin fields. Judging from the number of cars in the parking lot, Andy Brown was certainly doing something right.

Opening the car door, Lucy heard recorded wails and shrieks, punctuated by Vincent Price's voice.

"It's the Monster Mash," a delighted Elizabeth cried.

"Hurry up, Mom," urged Toby. "We'll miss the wagon."

"There'll be another one," said Sue. "Your mom has to get Zoe and Sara."

After Lucy had zipped Zoe into the corduroy pouch, and released Sara from her booster seat, they all clustered around a bright orange post with a sign proclaiming PUMPKIN PATCH EXPRESS and waited for the wagon.

Soon one trundled and they were greeted by the cheery young driver.

"Climb on," he said. "I'm your driver, Brad, and we're off to the pumpkin patch!"

Lucy and Sue climbed on awkwardly and seated themselves on bales of hay, holding on for dear life as the wagon lurched into motion. The girls shrieked with excitement, even Toby was having a hard time maintaining the sophisticated, world-weary attitude he adopted when he was out in public with his mother.

"Now, when you see the pumpkin you want, don't hesitate to holler. We can stop as often as you want," advised Brad.

"We want a perfeck pumpkin," piped up Sara.

"Well, you've come to the right place," said Brad. "We've got twenty acres of pumpkins. This is the biggest pick-your-own pumkin patch in the state of Maine, maybe in the entire United States."

"I don't doubt it," said Lucy. "What do you think of that one, over there?"

"Ick," said Elizabeth. "I want a round pumpkin. That's a tall pumpkin."

"There's a nice round one," said Sue. "See it?"

"That's too small," said Toby.

"I don't know if we have room in the car for a really big one, Toby," reminded Lucy.

"That's it!" shrieked Sara. They followed her little pointed finger, and spotted a lovely, round pumpkin.

"Stop!" Toby bellowed, jumping off the wagon and leaping over pumpkins and vines. He hoisted the pumpkin in triumph, and then dropped it. "Uggh," he exclaimed. "It was all squishy."

"Sometimes they get that way," Brad admitted.

"What about that one next to it?" Lucy asked.

Toby approached it cautiously. "It looks okay."

"Knock on it," Lucy said.

Toby gave it a rap; it sounded like he was knocking on a door.

"Bring it over," Lucy ordered, with a wave. Seeing Toby struggle, Brad jumped down to help him lift the pumpkin and hoist it onto the wagon.

"That looks good, what do you think? Besides, it's getting cold."

"Hot chocolate, cider, and donuts inside," Brad recited, climbing back onto his seat and setting the tractor in motion. "Also, don't miss the chance to visit the House of Horror. Today, we also have a pumpkin carving seminar with lifestyles expert Corney Clark."

"Sue, don't you want to get a pumpkin?" Lucy asked.

"I'm going to get a white one. They have them inside."

"I never heard of such a thing."

"I saw them in a magazine," Sue explained. "You carve them with an Exacto knife. Something a little different, more like a lantern."

"Really?" Lucy was skeptical, as she climbed down from the wagon and followed Brad to the cashier's counter. "I guess we'll stick with the traditional version. How much do I owe you?" She asked the cashier.

"Sixteen dollars and forty-two cents."

"Are you sure?"

The cashier nodded her head. "Yes. It weighs thirty-three and a half pounds, at forty-nine cents a pound."

"Okay," Lucy agreed. This was highway robbery, but she couldn't disappoint the kids. "Will you take a check?"

"Certainly. We also accept Visa, Mastercard, and American Express."

"Cancel that sale," said Andy Brown, materializing behind the cashier. "Bill Stone's money isn't any good here," he said, with a big smile and a wink.

"What do you mean?" asked Lucy, puzzled.

"A free pumpkin's the least I can do for my buddy Bill," said Andy. "Just to let him know there's no hard feelings because he voted against my sign."

"Oh," said Lucy, as the light dawned. Andy was offering a small bribe because Bill was on the commission. "There was nothing personal in his vote. Bill will always vote his conscience, you know." She reopened her checkbook. "Now, how much was that pumpkin? Sixteen forty-two?"

Andy shrugged, and nodded to the cashier, who rang up the sale.

"I'm hungry," Elizabeth said, with a meaningful glance at the snack bar in the corner.

"Here's five dollars," Lucy said. "You guys get what you want. I'm going to watch this demonstration with Sue."

She waited a minute to make sure that Toby and Elizabeth didn't run off without Sara, and then joined the group of women clustered around Corney Clarke.

———

"We don't need to carve pumpkins a certain way, just because we've always done it that way," advised Corney, with a flip of her blond pageboy. "Pumpkin carving is yet another opportunity to explore our creativity, to express ourselves, each in our own unique way."

Zoe was getting restless in the pouch, so Lucy began rocking her back and forth, while she listened to Corney.

"You might choose to express your feminine side, your love of lace and crystal, with a white pumpkin like this." Corney displayed an intricately carved creation that looked more like a piece of delicate porcelain than a pumpkin. The women oohed.

"Or perhaps you'd like to express your whacky sense of humor," said Corney, grinning mischievously. She uncovered an enormous blue hubbard squash, with B-O-O carved in it. The last O contained the small figure of a ghost. The women chuckled.

"Or, perhaps you really want to scare someone." Corney paused dramatically, then uncovered a pumpkin with a spider carved into its side. Little black plastic spiders had been artistically placed to augment the effect. The women squealed.

"As you can see, there is no right way to carve a pumpkin." Corney leaned forward and nodded reassuringly at the women. "There is only the way that is right for you. You must reach deep down inside yourself and find the wellsprings of your creativity. Then, you must look at your pumpkin. Go beyond the surface. Release the spirit within your gourd."

A wail from Zoe broke the awed silence with which the women were receiving Corney's every word. Lucy decided it was time for a strategic retreat.

"Catch you later," she told Sue, and headed over to the snack bar.

"Coffee, black," she told the girl behind the counter. Then, carrying her cup over to a table, she joined the kids, discreetly lifting her sweater so Zoe could have a snack, too.

"Whaddya think, guys," she observed, taking in the elaborate decorations and the frenzied commercialization of Farmer Brown's farmstand, "Is it me, or is Halloween getting out of control?"

CHAPTER NINETEEN

Later that evening, after supper, Lucy wondered if she had been too hasty when she encouraged Bill to go to Shelburne Village. Maybe I should have fallen on my knees and begged him to stay home, thought Lucy, plunging her arm up to the elbow in pumpkin guts.

"It's a shame Dad's missing this," she told the kids, who were gathered around the newspaper-covered kitchen table. "He would've loved it."

"We didn't wanna wait," Toby said. "It's almost Halloween."

"Only four more days," Elizabeth said.

"I can't wait," Sara squealed. "Trick or treat!"

Propped in her baby seat, Zoe did not seem very excited about pumpkin carving, or Halloween. If anything, her expression seemed to indicate some internal discomfort. She gave a little hiccup, and then started to cry.

"I have to feed the baby. Toby, can you finish cleaning out this pumpkin?"

"Sure." He started to reach into the pumpkin.

"Roll your sleeves up," Lucy advised.

"Oh, yeah."

Lucy kept an eye on him as she rinsed her hands, dried them, and picked up the baby. "No funny stuff," she warned, just as he picked up a handful of stringy seeds and hurled them at Elizabeth.

"That's it," she told Elizabeth, who was scooping up a handful herself in order to retaliate. "It stops here."

"That's not fair! He gets away with everything!"

"He's not getting away with it. I'll punish him later. Right now, let's concentrate on finishing up this pumpkin."

"How are you going to punish him?" asked Elizabeth, as Lucy settled Zoe at her breast.

"I don't know. I'll think of something."

"You should ground him," Elizabeth suggested with a malicious grin.

"That's not fair! You get grounded for something real bad, like stealing," Toby protested.

"I haven't decided, yet. Just remember, you owe a debt to society, young man. So, what kind of eyes are you going to give it?"

"Two triangles," said Sara.

"You don't have to make triangles. You can be creative. How about big, spooky circles?"

"Triangles," Toby said.

"Triangles," Elizabeth agreed.

Lucy sighed. "Okay, make triangles." Sometimes Lucy wondered about her children. They were so conservative. They never wanted to try anything new. "Be careful with that knife, Toby."

"How do you want the nose?" Toby asked. "Triangle?"

"Triangle," Sara said.

"Triangle," Elizabeth agreed.

"You know, I saw somewhere, how they made the pumpkin seeds dribble out of the jack-o'-lantern's mouth, so it looked like throw up," Lucy suggested, propping Zoe on her shoulder and patting her back. "It looked kinda neat, if you like that sort of thing."

"Yuck," Toby said, grimacing.

"That's disgusting," Elizabeth observed, as Zoe upchucked all over Lucy's shoulder.

"It's only spit up," said Lucy. "I hope she isn't coming down with something."

"She sure knows how to come up with something," volunteered Toby, pleased at his cleverness.

"Make the mouth smile," Sara said.

"A big grin with lots of teeth," Elizabeth added.

"What did you think of Mrs. Finch's white pumpkin?" Lucy asked, gently rocking Zoe.

"It's just not Halloween," said Elizabeth. "This pumpkin's right for Halloween."

Toby placed a flashlight inside the pumpkin and turned it on. Then he switched off the kitchen light, and they all admired the jack-o'-lantern. It had two triangle eyes, a triangle nose, and a big toothy grin. It was perfect.

"Okay, Toby. For punishment you can clean up. I'm going to put Zoe in her crib and see if she'll go to sleep."

"Aw, Mom, do I have to?"

"Yes, you have to. If you throw stuff around and make a mess, you get to clean it up. That's how it works, and I don't want to hear another word about it."

Surprised at her tone, Toby glanced at his mother. Lucy raised her eyebrows, and he decided that further argument would not be in his best interest. Instead, he reached for a sponge.

Coming back downstairs, Lucy listened to Zoe's crying and wiped up the table. Toby had done his best, it was just that when Toby cleaned up, somebody had to clean up after him. The baby wasn't really wailing, her crying was more in the nature of a complaint. Lucy decided to wait a bit and see if she'd go to sleep, so she opened the refrigerator and pulled out the salad greens.

Even after she'd made the salad, and boiled the water for the macaroni, Zoe was still crying.

"Elizabeth, could you get the baby? I'm making supper."

"Do I have to?"

"Yes. You can sit in the rocking chair with her."

"What if she throws up on me?"

"Then we'll clean you up. Do you want to eat tonight? I can cook, or I can rock the baby."

"I have to do everything around here," Elizabeth complained, mounting the stairs.

"Right," said Lucy, mixing up the cheesy sauce. "She has to do everything."

"Mom, the baby feels hot," Elizabeth said, when she returned to the kitchen with the baby.

"She's been crying," said Lucy, bending down to kiss Zoe's forehead. "Maybe she has a little fever."

"What if she's sick?"

"I'll get a cool washcloth. You can wipe her face, see if she cools down."

All through supper, which they ate in front of the TV as a special treat, Lucy laughed along with the kids at a silly sitcom rerun and refused to admit how worried she was about the baby. Zoe wasn't interested in nursing and only stopped wailing when Lucy held her against her shoulder. Finally, Lucy gave her a tiny dose of fever medicine, and she drifted off to sleep.

Returning to the kitchen, Lucy loaded the dishwasher and wiped off the counter. Then, deciding she still had a tiny bit of energy left, she mixed up another two dozen cupcakes and set them in the oven. While they baked, she thought about calling the doctor.

No point, she decided, at this hour she would only get the answering service. Zoe probably had a little cold, nothing to worry about. She was well-nourished, well-hydrated, full of maternal antibodies. If she wasn't better tomorrow morning, Lucy decided, she'd call the doctor then.

By the time Lucy got the older kids settled down, and had changed into her nightclothes herself, it was ten o'clock. Zoe kept waking and fussing, nursing a bit and spitting up. Lucy tried bathing her to bring down the fever, but Zoe cried so much she abandoned the idea. Dressing her only in a diaper and shirt and wrapping her in a light receiving blanket, Lucy held her against her shoulder, and sat in the rocking chair. Rocking was the only thing that seemed to soothe the baby, which meant going to bed was out of the question.

Lucy rocked back and forth. She listened to the dishwasher go through its cycle. She listened to the hum of the refrigerator. She heard the click of the thermostat, and the whoosh of the furnace. She closed her eyes and told herself that resting was almost the same as sleeping.

A second later the phone rang.

Startled, she jumped to her feet, clutching the baby. She picked up the receiver.

"Hello," she said, expecting to hear Bill's voice.

She didn't hear anything, just the sound of someone breathing. That was followed by a hoarse, male voice. "You can't stop me."

Then, far away in the distance, she heard the fire horn, and the wail of sirens.

CHAPTER TWENTY

Had he made a fool of himself? Driving back home the next afternoon, Bill wasn't sure. This consultant stuff was harder than he had expected. He hoped the Shelburne Village people weren't disappointed in him.

He'd done his best. The door was atypical. Quite unique. He'd never seen anything like it. Some features were eighteenth century, others nineteenth. Faced with the curator's puzzled expression, he'd finally ventured a guess that it was made in the nineteenth century by a very old craftsman using his father's tools.

It wasn't that far-fetched, he told himself. Even today, in remote pockets of New England, there were people repairing chairs and building stone walls and making baskets just the way their parents or grandparents had taught them.

Turning onto Main Street, he sighed. No use crying over spilt milk. What was done was done. Either they were impressed with his honesty and frankness, or they figured he was a fool. In the big scheme of things it hardly mattered. He had plenty of work to keep him busy and put food on the family table.

Slowing for a traffic tie-up, Bill was surprised to see a cop directing traffic. Given the time of year, Tinker's Cove only had traffic problems in the summer, this was unusual. Curious, he pulled over and got out of his truck. He had only gone a few feet down Main Street when he saw the blackened remains of Doug Durning's real estate office.

"What the hell," he said under his breath, joining the group of curious onlookers along the yellow tape.

"Our arsonist at work again," said Ted Stillings, returning his camera to its case.

"When did it happen?"

"Last night. It was some blaze. Chief called for mutual aid from companies as far away as Gilead and Wilton. Twelve engines, thirty-five firefighters, it was quite a show. Where were you?"

"I had business over in Vermont. I'm just getting back." Bill shook his head. "This is an awful shame. That was a nice old house."

"Yeah. *Was* is the operative word. Chief says it's a complete loss. There's Doug, now. Excuse me, I've got to get a statement."

Bill watched as Ted approached Doug, notebook in hand.

"I'm sorry to bother you at a time like this," he began. "I just wondered if you have anything to say for *The Pennysaver?*"

"I sure do," Doug began. "I'm mad as hell." His face was red and his gestures were choppy. Bill wondered if he'd been drinking; he wouldn't have blamed him if he had. "What's it gonna take? How many buildings have to burn before they catch this guy? Is he gonna burn the whole goddam town down before they get him?"

Suddenly deflated, Doug paused for breath and staggered. Ted took him by the arm and steadied him.

"This was my life," he said, shaking his head. "I took some hits in the recession, but business was picking up. I was one of the survivors—I thought. Now it's all gone. I've lost everything."

"Was the building insured?" asked Ted, scribbling away.

"Yeah, but not enough. Not near enough. I'd cut back, trying to save money."

"That's too bad," said Ted, momentarily at a loss for words. He always found it hard not to identify with the people he interviewed, and this cut close to the bone. He could put himself in Doug's place all too easily, and knew how devastated he'd be if the Pennysaver Press burned. "Hang in there, man," he said, giving Doug a pat on the shoulder.

Standing a few feet away, Bill also sympathized with Doug.

"I'm sorry," he said, stepping up and clasping his hand. "Anything I can do?"

Doug stared hollowly at the burned-out building that had been his livelihood, and gestured emptily with his hands. Blinking furiously, he turned away and headed down the street. Bill watched him go, then climbed in his truck.

It was time to go home.

When he pulled into his own driveway, however, he was surprised to see a police cruiser parked by the back door. Hurrying into the kitchen he was relieved to see it was only Barney, sitting at the kitchen table with a mug of coffee.

"Hi," he said, pouring himself a cup, giving Lucy a peck on the cheek and joining them at the table. "Guess you guys were busy last night, hunh?"

"You could say that," agreed Barney.

"I saw Doug. He's taking it pretty hard."

"I was just there the other day. I was thinking what a nice old place it is . . . was," said Lucy.

"I gotta finish this report, Lucy," Barney said, reluctantly drawing her attention to the form on the table in front of him.

"There isn't much to tell," Lucy began. "The phone rang around ten. I picked it up. There was a breathing sound, then someone said, 'You can't stop me.' Then I heard the sirens."

"When was this?" demanded Bill.

"Last night."

"Are you telling me the arsonist called here?" demanded Bill, looking at Barney.

"We don't know who called," admitted Barney. "The timing could have been a coincidence."

Bill turned to face Lucy. "How come you didn't call the police right away? Why'd you wait til now?"

"Calm down," she said. "I called first thing this morning and Barney got here as soon as he could. I thought about calling last night, but I could hear the fire horn and I knew everybody'd be busy. It wasn't an emergency—it was just a phone call. A scary phone call. I figured it was a Halloween prank, like the paint on the car. Actually, I was more worried about the baby."

"What's the matter with the baby?"

"Ear infection. I took her to the doctor this morning. She'll be fine."

"I hate this," said Bill, fingering his coffee mug. "I go away for one night and all hell breaks loose."

"Not quite," said Lucy, patting his hand.

"What did he say? It was a man?"

"Definitely a man. He said, 'You can't stop me.' "

"Have you made any enemies lately?" asked Barney. "Had an argument with someone, made anybody angry?"

"It's the commission," said Bill, smacking his forehead with his hand. "I never should've agreed to join that thing. Doug's a member, and look what happened to him. All you do is make people mad. The couple with the green house, Andy Brown, Lenk—any one of them could be pissed off at me."

"Not the couple," said Lucy.

"Right. I voted for them."

"People do take this stuff more seriously than I thought," said Lucy, thinking of the free pumpkin Andy Brown had offered her.

"Sure they do," said Bill. "That commission is powerful. If I had to paint my house all over again, I might make an anonymous phone call or two myself. Maybe I'd even be mad enough to set a fire."

"Hold your horses, Bill. You're kinda jumping to conclusions, here. We don't know who made the call," said Barney. "Most likely Lucy's right and it's a Halloween trick."

"Arson and anonymous phone calls kind of go together," said Lucy, thinking of the description of the typical arsonist in the psychology book. She had been so sure that Krissy and Dr. Mayes were responsible for the fires, now she wasn't so certain. Maybe there was a pyromaniac loose in Tinker's Cove.

Or, maybe that's exactly what Krissy and Dr. Mayes hoped everyone would think. Maybe this fire was carefully planned to divert attention away from Monica and bolster the theory that she was truly a hapless victim who was just in the wrong place at the wrong time.

Or, thought Lucy, her mind racing, maybe the fire was supposed to send a message to Doug. Did he know something he shouldn't? Had he stumbled on some bit of evidence? Did they need to get him out of the way, too? Lucy's heart skipped a beat. What if they knew she suspected them and had been asking questions? Would they come after her next?

"Are you okay?" Bill asked, interrupting her thought. "You're awfully quiet."

"You look kinda pale, Lucy." Barney furrowed his brow in concern, looking a bit like a huge St. Bernard.

"Maybe this is more serious than I thought," Lucy admitted. "The paint, the phone call—maybe somebody is trying to warn me off."

"What do you mean, Lucy?" Bill asked. "Warn you off what?"

Lucy held her breath, waiting for Bill to draw the inevitable conclusion.

"Have you been investigating these fires?" Bill looked her right in the eye.

Lucy looked at the salt and pepper shakers on the table. "Not really."

"What does 'not really' mean?"

"I think . . . I thought it might have been Dr. Mayes, especially after I learned about him and Krissy. I was asking some questions around the gym."

"I wish you'd mind your own business, Lucy," said Bill.

"You should leave this investigation to the police," advised Barney.

United in agreement, Bill and Barney sat back and lifted their coffee mugs.

"What about those Patriots?" began Bill.

"I think I hear the baby," said Lucy, glad to escape the male chauvinists in the kitchen. But as she tended to the baby one fact became very clear to her. If the arsonist was threatening her there was only one thing she could do. She had to catch him before he had a chance to hurt her, or her family.

As much as she liked Barney, she had to admit he didn't exactly inspire confidence in the investigative abilities of the Tinker's Cove Police Department. It was time to consult an expert. Fortunately, she had made the acquaintance of a state police detective a few years ago when she was working for the Country Cousins catalog store and found the body of the owner, Sam Miller, in the parking lot. She decided to give Detective Horowitz a call.

CHAPTER TWENTY-ONE

Glancing around the kitchen the next afternoon, Lucy wondered how things had degenerated so fast. The sink and counter were littered with dirty dishes, the garbage bin was overflowing, the tablecloth was stained and full of crumbs. Was it just a few days ago that she had been congratulating herself on managing so well?

It was the cupcakes, she decided. Twelve dozen cupcakes was the straw that broke the camel's back. If it wasn't for the damned cupcakes, she told herself as she reached for a bowl and box of cake mix, she would have time for everything else. At least she had reached the halfway mark—when these were done she would only have six dozen to go. Six dozen, three more days until Halloween, that was two dozen a day. No problem. The trick, of course, was to keep the kids from finding them. That's why she had to get this batch baked, cooled, iced, and hidden on the top shelf of the pantry before the school bus arrived. It was one o'clock—she had almost two hours, plenty of time as long as Zoe didn't wake up early from her nap.

Hearing the crunch of tires on the gravel driveway, Lucy went to the window to see who it was. Seeing the familiar unmarked blue Ford, Lucy smiled. Detective Horowitz was as good as his word.

"Hi," she said, opening the door for him. "It's good to see you—it's been a while."

"That's right, Mrs. Stone." Horowitz was a serious, formal man with a long face and rabbit lips. He always looked tired.

"Can I get you some coffee?"

"No, thanks. If I have too much I can't sleep at night." He pulled out a chair to sit down, and picked up the large sneaker that was resting on it.

Lucy took it from him, and tossed it in the corner next to its mate. "Toby—he's eleven."

"Big feet," he said, sitting down heavily.

"You detectives are so observant." Lucy took a seat at the table opposite him.

"It's our job, ma'am," said Horowitz, with the slightest hint of a smile. "So what seems to be the trouble?"

"You know about the fires? Are you working on them?"

"Not directly, but I'm familiar with the case."

"Well, I'm worried someone may be threatening me—but maybe it's just Halloween. There was paint on my car, I got a phone call, and I found this in my mailbox this morning." She slipped a small piece of paper across the table.

Horowitz looked down at it, but didn't touch it. It was a piece of cheap, lined notepaper crudely ripped from a spiral pad. Little square bits of paper clung to the top, and the right corner was missing. A black marker pen had been used to write the brief message in childish block letters: MIND YOUR OWN BIZNESS OR BURN.

"Have you been investigating the fires?" he asked, raising his pale eyes to meet hers.

"A little bit here and there—I don't have much time. I have a new baby, you know." Lucy stood up. "Do you mind if I do some cooking? I have to bake some cupcakes for a Halloween party."

"Not at all." Horowitz studied the note. "What are your thoughts on the fires, Mrs. Stone?"

"I'm no expert," began Lucy, switching on the oven and setting paper liners in the cupcake pans. "I don't know anything about accelerants or stuff like that, but I can't help thinking Dr. Mayes had an awful lot to gain from burning down the Homestead." Lucy paused and began ripping open the box of cake mix.

"Go on."

"He got rid of his wife, no divorce, no alimony, and he'll get a big insurance settlement. You know about the girlfriend, right?"

Horowitz nodded.

"So you agree with me? He is a suspect then?"

"Was. He couldn't have done it."

"What about Krissy? They're more than lovers, you know. He owns part of her business."

Horowitz looked interested, in spite of himself.

"You didn't know that, did you?" crowed Lucy.

"I told you, I'm not directly involved in this case. But I hadn't heard that. Are you sure?"

"Yup." Lucy cracked an egg on the side of the bowl. "She told me herself. I joined the gym, you know, to get back in shape after the baby." She switched on the mixer.

"I'll pass it along," promised Horowitz. "Mind if I take the note?"

"Please. I'll be glad to get rid of it."

"Did you handle it much?" he asked, slipping it carefully into a plastic bag.

"Probably. It was under the mail. I flipped through the letters and stuff before I even found it."

"I don't think this note is connected with the fires," said Horowitz.

"Why do you say that?" asked Lucy carefully, pouring the batter into the cupcake pans. Then she slid the pans into the oven.

"The only reason I'm telling you this is because I don't want you to worry. They're very close to making an arrest in this case. I'm no expert in accelerants either, but they tell me that the same accelerant was used in every fire. They're all the work of the same individual, they know that because he has certain signature behaviors. He doesn't write notes." Horowitz took a packet of photographs from his pocket. "These are between you and me and nobody else, okay?"

Lucy nodded eagerly and leaned across the table.

"Fire one, the theater." He spread out three or four photos.

Lucy was shocked and fascinated by what she saw. A row of red plush theater seats with blackened, burned centers. A cot in a dressing room, covered by a neat plaid spread. Only the center was burned. The stage, completely ruined by flames.

"You can see how he splashed accelerant around, but not enough to do the job. Real amateur. He did better with the barn."

Horowitz handed her another photograph. This one showed the one remaining corner of the barn, the wood blistered and scarred by the fire.

"This time he used enough accelerant. The conditions were in his favor. The wood was old and dry, there hadn't been rain for a couple of weeks. The barn was a total loss. Not the powder house. It was barely touched," he said, passing her another photo. "Too public, he probably got scared away. Then the Homestead, and Durning's place." He flipped down the photos as if he were dealing cards. "He's hit his stride. He knows what he's doing. Complete losses, both of them. He probably thinks there wasn't any evidence left, but there was. A lot of evidence. The lab guys are real happy with this one. I wouldn't worry if I were you. This guy doesn't write notes or make phone calls or anything like that. All he cares about is making a nice, big fire."

"This is creepy," said Lucy, gathering up the pictures and handing them back to Horowitz. "He's crazy."

"A sick puppy. But he's not Dr. Mayes, and he's not Dr. Mayes's girlfriend whatever her name is, and he's probably not even aware of your existence so don't worry anymore, okay?"

"Okay," said Lucy, opening the door for him.

"On the other hand, I wouldn't dismiss this note," he said, patting his pocket. "It's pretty good advice, if you ask me. Leave the investigating to the experts, Mrs. Stone." He paused and sniffed, wrinkling his nose. "Do I smell something burning?"

"The cupcakes!" cried Lucy, dashing for the oven.

CHAPTER TWENTY-TWO

"What happened to you?"

Slipping into a seat beside Sue at the TCHDC hearing Thursday evening, Lucy couldn't help noticing the Band-Aids on her fingers.

"I'm a victim of Corney Clarke."

"Corney Clarke did that to you?"

"Not directly. I did it to myself. I was overambitious. I reached for the stars. I wasn't happy to have a regular orange jack-o'-lantern like everybody else. Oh no. I had to have a white pumpkin, artistically carved to look like lace."

"It was tougher than you thought."

"I'll say. The damn thing was like cement. I used Sid's wood-carving tools, but I couldn't make a dent in it. I sure made a mess of my hands, though."

"That's terrible," said Lucy, unable to control her laughter as she pictured Sue hacking away at the little white pumpkin.

"It's not funny," Sue sniffed indignantly. "I could've bled to death or lost a finger."

"I'm sorry," Lucy said, adopting a serious tone. "I guess the spirit of your gourd wasn't ready to be released yet."

"You could say that gourd was not afraid to defend itself," Sue said. "It was one spirited squash. But I got it in the end."

"You did?"

"I ran over it."

"With the car?" Lucy asked incredulously.

Sue nodded her head proudly. "Yup."

"Didn't that make an awful mess?"

"Sure did. I'm not proud of it, but I did it. I squashed that squash."

"This hearing will now come to order," announced Miss Tilley with a bang of her gavel.

Silence was not immediate. The hearing room was packed and it took a while for everyone to quiet down. In addition to Ted, the cable TV station had sent a crew, and several local radio station reporters were also present. Such extensive coverage wasn't really necessary; it seemed that everyone who was interested was already there.

"This is a public hearing on the application of Randolph Lenk for a certificate of appropriateness for alterations to an existing structure in the Tinker's Cove Historic District. Mr. Lenk, I understand you have legal representation tonight?"

"Whuh," said Lenk, arching an eyebrow. He hadn't gone to any trouble for the hearing. He was dressed in his usual grimy work clothes, and had a two-day stubble of beard.

"I am representing Mr. Lenk," volunteered a tall young man

dressed in a pin stripe suit. "I am Fred Carruthers from the legal department at Northstar. I would also like to introduce Dave Anderson, vice-president in charge of development, New England, Stan Lepke, head of our design department, and Cindy Josephs, from our public relations department."

The three didn't need to stand. Their sober business suits and professional demeanor set them apart from everyone else in the room. Cindy smiled brightly, but it was clear that she was a strange fish in these waters, with her crisp navy suit, panty hose, heels, and perfectly coiffed hair.

"Can you imagine dressing like that?" whispered Lucy, crossing her blue jean-clad legs.

"Only for a funeral," answered Sue, slipping out of her barn jacket.

"I understand you have a presentation," Miss Tilley said, once again banging her gavel for order.

"That's right," Carruthers answered. "First, we have a brief history on the development of the concept. Dave Anderson will handle that."

"If I may," said Mr. Anderson, stepping forward. He shifted his shoulders in his navy jacket, and smoothed his red print tie.

"The design we are proposing for Mr. Lenk's station was developed in response to several factors." He walked over to an easel set to one side and pointed to an architect's drawing of a futuristic gas station.

"First, we must meet federal and state safety requirements. This is not voluntary. We must have a vapor recovery system and a fire suppression system." He waved a laser pointer in the direction of the canopy.

"Second, as a business, we are interested in responding to the expressed needs and demands of our customers. Consumer polls tell us that our customers want self-service pumps that accept charge cards. They want to get their gas and get back on the road as fast as they can." He pointed to the gas pump.

"Convenience is important to our consumers. They appreciate being able to pick up cigarettes, a gallon of milk, a cup of coffee, when they get gas. So, we've added convenience markets to our stations to meet that need.

"We have also added complimentary car washes. This is a feature consumers really appreciate—a free car wash with a purchase of eight or more gallons. This is especially popular in northern areas like yours. I don't have to tell you the damage road salt can do to the finish on your cars and trucks.

"I'm giving you this background so you'll understand some of the factors that led to the development of this particular design. Now, I'm going to turn things over to Stan."

Stan Lepke stood up and approached the easel. He was a few inches shorter than Dave Anderson, his hair a few shades lighter. He, too, shifted his shoulders in his dark gray jacket and smoothed his red print tie.

"This design," he began, indicating the easel, "is something Northstar is very proud of. We believe it combines form and function in the best tradition of modern design, meets all safety regulations, and is appealing and attractive to customers.

"Furthermore, we have adapted this design to complement the architectural styles of the various regions of our great country."

He flipped a page. "In the Southwest we use simulated stucco."

He turned the page. "In the Pacific Northwest, notice the totem pole theme.

"On the next illustration, we show the barn theme used in the Midwest. In the South, these one hundred percent vinyl pillars are reminiscent of the great plantations. And here in the Northeast, you'll notice I've saved the best for last, our simulated clapboard and cedar shingles are almost indistinguishable from the real thing."

"Why don't you use the real thing?" came a voice from the audience. There was a murmur of agreement from the crowd.

"Order," said Miss Tilley, banging down her gavel. "We will take questions from the floor later. Right now, if you are done, Mr. Lepke, I think the board has some questions for you."

"Fine," said Mr. Lepke. "I may not have all the answers but I'll do my best."

"I have a question," said Bill. "I think the man in the audience had a valid point. Why don't you use real clapboard and cedar shingles?"

"Maintenance," answered Mr. Lepke. "Gas stations are dirty, it's a dirty business. Car exhaust, road dirt, you know what I'm talking about. These simulated materials can be washed and hosed down."

"Why does the station need to be so large?" asked Miss Tilley. "Mr. Lenk's present station is often empty, and he has two pumps. Why do you need to add six more?"

"I'll pass that question on to Mr. Anderson," said Mr. Lepke.

"That is a good question," began Mr. Anderson. "It comes to me because as vice-president responsible for development, it has fallen to my division to implement our corporation's strategic plan for right-sizing. To boil down this rather complicated effort to maximize profit and improve service, we are reducing the number of service sites in this particular facet of the corporate structure." He blinked furiously as he ended his spiel.

"If I understand you correctly," said Hancock Smith, a retired corporate vice-president himself, "Northstar is closing a number of stations, hoping to redirect business to a smaller number of better-equipped stations?"

"That's right." Mr. Anderson swallowed hard, and smoothed his tie.

"So Mr. Lenk's station has been chosen for improvements, while other Northstar stations in surrounding towns will be closed?"

"Right, again." Mr. Anderson nodded his agreement.

"That will mean increased traffic," observed Miss Tilley.

"Increased traffic is not necessarily bad," observed Jock Mulligan. "It could bring more people to the other businesses in town. People have to come to get gas, so they also do their grocery shopping or banking. However, I do have r-real r-r-reservations about this design. It's absolutely atrocious."

"I tend to agree," said Bill. "This is an historic area, and this design looks like a misplaced space station."

"I think we've heard from everyone except Mr. Durning," said Miss Tilley. "Do you have anything to add, Doug?"

Doug, who had been listlessly shuffling through his packet of papers throughout the meeting, shook his head.

"I will now open this up to the floor," said Miss Tilley. "The chair recognizes Fred Tibbett."

Fred, a gray-haired man dressed in the Tinker's Cove uniform of khaki pants, plaid flannel shirt, and windbreaker, stood up.

"Goes to reason," he said, "if you fellas are investin' a whole lotta money in this here station, you'll wanna get some kind o' return. Does that mean you'll be raisin' the price of gas?"

"I guess that question is for me," said Cindy Josephs, jumping to her feet. She shifted her shoulders inside her neat navy jacket and tossed her blond hair.

"The price of Northstar gas is figured based on a number of factors that include our costs, taxes, the price our competitors are charging, and what we call the value factor. That is, what consumers are willing to pay for our particular gasoline. Have I made myself clear?"

"Nope," said Fred.

"What she's trying to say, or trying not to say, is that if they think they can get more, they'll charge more," said Hancock Smith, much to the amusement of the crowd. Cindy shrugged and sat down.

"The chair recognizes Dotty Cooper," said Miss Tilley.

Mrs. Cooper, a gray-haired woman dressed in wool slacks and a sweater, stood up.

"As most of you know, I live opposite Mr. Lenk's station. I have no problem with the station as it is now. It's a quiet little country gas station. I get gas there myself. Mr. Lenk is open from seven or so in the morning until six in the evening, he's not open at night. If my guess is right, this thing will be brightly lit twenty-four hours a day and all sorts of people will be coming at all hours of the day and night. I really object to it. I think it would have a negative effect on the neighborhood."

"Very well said, Dotty. You can be sure the board will take your comments very seriously." Miss Tilley nodded her head and banged down her gavel. "Joe Marzetti."

"You all know me," began Joe, the owner of the local IGA. "For more years than I like to count I've been doing my best to provide good food at good prices. I'm the only grocery store in Tinker's Cove—if I went out of business you'd have to go quite some ways to the superstore. I'm telling you, I'm not getting rich at this. There's not a heck of a lot of business in this town, especially in the winter. What I don't need is a gas station cutting into my milk and bread business—I think Northstar should stick to selling gas."

Miss Tilley nodded and recognized Jonathan Franke, executive director of APTC—the Association for the Preservation of Tinker's Cove.

"I see a lot of APTC members here tonight," began Franke. He had recently trimmed the wild beard and long hair that had been his signature in favor of a more conservative, professional look. "In the past few years I think there's been a recognition that the environment is the basis of our economy here. Let's face it, people are not going to come and vacation here if the water is polluted and the trees are all dead. My concern about the Northstar plan is the proposed car wash. If a car wash is to be included, we have to make sure that the water is recycled, and that any runoff is contained and treated appropriately before it is allowed to return to the aquifer. This water could be a real toxic brew."

"I would like to answer that," said Mr. Carruthers, rising to his feet. "You can be sure that Northstar will comply with all EPA regulations. We are as concerned about the environment as you are—we all share the same planet."

"Then why does your company routinely use single-hulled tankers?" demanded Franke. "What about the North Sea oil spill? You had no part in that? You're still fighting for reduced damages in court!"

The gavel came down. "Thank you, Mr. Franke. You can be sure we all appreciate your efforts on our behalf," said Miss Tilley.

"Are there any more questions?" She scanned the audience, apparently failing to see a number of raised hands. "Since there are no more questions, I would like to suggest a course of action for this commission. I propose we continue this hearing to a later date. Furthermore, I suggest Northstar withdraw their application without prejudice, and come back with a more appropriate plan. Is everyone agreed?"

Seeing no disagreement, Miss Tilley continued, shaking a

bony finger at the corporate executives. "It's obvious this plan simply will not do. Not in Tinker's Cove. I suggest you gentlefolk go back to the drawing board. Surely a company with your resources can come up with something simple, unobtrusive, and tasteful. Here in New England, we are proud of our heritage. We value the buildings constructed by our ancestors, we still hold the same values they did. We have a sense of place. We don't want to look like New Jersey, do we?"

"Hey, what's this mean? You tellin' me I can't fix up my station?" Randy Lenk was on his feet, gesturing angrily with his fists.

"Mr. Lenk, I have explained this to you before. Your station is in the historic district. You can make alterations, but they must be approved beforehand by the historic commission—that is this board. If your proposal is approved by this group of five people you see sitting here tonight, then you can go ahead." Miss Tilley spoke clearly and slowly, as if to a first-grader who insisted on talking in the library.

"Has it been approved?" asked Lenk.

"No, it hasn't."

"Well, take a vote right now. I want it approved."

"We understand that. However, Mr. Lenk, the proposal we saw tonight does not stand the least chance of being approved by this board. You have heard the expression about an ice cube in hell? This proposal has less chance than that. However, we are allowing you to withdraw this proposal without prejudice, and come back with a new one. We're doing you a very big favor."

"You're not doing me any favor," he shouted angrily. "Who do you think you are? I can do what I want with my land. You can't stop me. It's mine. I can do whatever I damn well please with it. Ain't that right?"

Lucy jerked to attention. What was that Lenk had said? *You can't stop me.*

Miss Tilley banged down her gavel. "Do I hear a motion to adjourn?"

Wasn't that what the anonymous phone caller had said? While the board went through the business of voting to adjourn, Lucy studied Randolph Lenk. Was he the one who made the phone call?

She grimaced with distaste as he ran his black, grimy fingers through his greasy hair and shook his fist at the board members. "It's my property," he yelled, revealing uneven broken teeth. "I can do what I want!"

"Meeting adjourned," announced Miss Tilley, pointedly ignoring him and banging down the gavel.

CHAPTER TWENTY-THREE

Driving home after the meeting, Lucy turned to Bill. "I think Randy Lenk made that anonymous phone call."

"I think so, too. Seems he called the other commission members. Said the same thing to everyone. 'You can't stop me.' "

Lucy shook her head. "What a weird thing to do."

"He's a pretty weird guy. You know that ugly sandpit on Bumps River Road."

"Mmm."

"That's his. It didn't used to be a pit like that. It was a nice piece of woods. He cut all the trees and stripped off the soil."

"Why would he do that?"

"Sold the timber and the top soil. Made a pretty penny, I guess. But he made the town so mad they passed a tree-cutting bylaw at the next town meeting. Now you have to get a permit from the conservation commission before you can clear-cut your property."

"That's good," Lucy said, nodding.

"Most people think so. But not Lenk. He was so mad he went out to another piece of land he owns—his family's been around forever and he's got a lot of land—and he ringed all the trees so they'd die. You've seen it, that sick-looking woods behind the dump."

"I thought it was toxic runoff from the dump or something."

"Nope. Lenk, making a point."

"Seems kind of crazy to me," Lucy said.

"Miss Tilley says it runs in the family," explained Bill. "According to her, his father was a pervert who got sent to jail and got himself killed. Apparently he set his bedding on fire as some sort of protest but nobody noticed until it was too late and he died. She said he died of stupidity."

"That's awful," Lucy said, wrapping her arms across her chest.

"Miss T. said it was the nicest thing he could have done for his family."

"She would." Lucy chuckled. "I wonder if he was a mental masturbator."

"You don't get sent to jail for crimes of the mind," said Bill, turning into the driveway and braking. He reached over and took Lucy's hand. "What did you think of your husband, the commissioner?"

"I thought you looked very handsome and important." Lucy squeezed his hand. "I was proud of you."

"I saw you, sitting next to Sue."

"Oh, yeah?" Lucy tilted her head. "What did you think?"

"I thought you looked pretty cute." He bent down and kissed her.

———————

When they went into the house a few minutes later, they found Jennifer sitting in the rocking chair with Zoe sound asleep in her arms.

"How did everything go?" asked Lucy.

"Fine. She took a little bit of the milk you left, but she didn't seem very hungry."

"She's still not quite herself. Did you give her the medicine?"

"Yup. Went down with no problem."

"You're amazing, Jennifer. It's wonderful to be able to go out for an evening and know the kids are in such capable hands."

"I love kids, especially babies," she said, carefully passing Zoe over to her mother.

"Can you sit for us a week from Saturday? I'll call with the details," asked Lucy, handing her a ten-dollar bill.

"Sure. I'll look forward to it," said Jennifer, bouncing out the door.

"Isn't she cute?" Lucy asked Bill. "She just got her driver's license—she's got a little car of her own. Wouldn't it be great to be sixteen again?"

"I remember my first car. It was a big old Dodge Dart. Gosh I had good times in that thing, until I hit an icy patch and slid into a light pole. I thought my father was going to kill me." He paused, and put down a stack of papers next to his chair. "There's something I want to check in the bylaws. I'll be up in a minute."

"Okay," said Lucy, taking the baby upstairs and gently placing her in her bassinet. Thoughtfully, she stroked Zoe's soft, fuzzy head with her index finger. She traced the roundness of her baby's head, and her cheek; she sniffed the sweet baby smell.

We all start out the same, she thought, how does a perfect little baby turn into a pathetic specimen like Randy Lenk? Once upon a time he must have been a lovely little baby. Though with a father like that, he certainly didn't get off to a very good start.

A pervert. Trust Miss Tilley to use a horrible word like that. An old-fashioned word. Today he'd be what? A child molester. An abusive parent. Lucy shuddered.

Suddenly, she wondered if Lenk could be the arsonist. Didn't he fit the profile in the psychology book? According to the learned author, arsonists frequently had difficulty accepting authority. They were often survivors of childhood sexual abuse. They also indulged in other antisocial behaviors, such as making anonymous telephone calls and writing hate letters. And even if he didn't have a justification for his behavior in the beginning, he certainly did now. He could have burned Doug's place as a warning to the other members of the historic commission.

Now that she thought about it, it seemed unlikely that Dr. Mayes was responsible for the fire at Doug's place. Having already achieved his objective, it would have been foolish and risky. Maybe Krissy did it, she thought, remembering how angry she had been with Dr. Mayes. Setting another fire would let him know that he couldn't control her, that she was dangerous when she didn't get what she wanted.

Lucy rubbed her temples. No doubt about it, she was getting a headache. She had been so sure that Dr. Mayes had set the fires but now she had her doubts. Instead of becoming clearer, this situation was getting murkier by the minute. She headed for the bathroom, thinking of a commercial for a painkiller she had seen on TV. "Yes," she said out loud to herself as she opened the medicine cabinet and reached for the familiar bottle, "I do get really tough headaches."

CHAPTER TWENTY-FOUR

The next morning, as soon as she had the house to herself, she picked up the phone and dialed. While it rang, she looked out the window at the red and yellow trees bordering the yard. She loved the way the garden looked in the fall, a bit tousled and blowsy, the sharp edges of summer blurred by frost. Brown leaves blew this way and that, the flowering annuals that had been so green and bright a few months ago now sprawled black and exhausted in their beds. She really needed to get out there with a rake and tidy up.

"Barney? I had an idea."

A low groan came through the receiver.

"Don't be like that. I think I may be on to something."

"Okay, shoot."

"Well, I think Randy Lenk might be the arsonist."

"Congratulations. You and everybody else."

"He was already a suspect?" Lucy was disappointed.

"You could say that. A prime suspect. Suspect number one."

"Well, how come he hasn't been arrested?" Lucy pulled a chair out from under the kitchen table and sat down, leaning her elbows on the table.

"He's been brought in for questioning, but we always had to let him go."

"Why?"

"Not enough evidence."

"Can't you stake him out or something?"

"We've been watching him, but somehow he always manages to slip away."

"That doesn't say much for the Tinker's Cove P.D.," Lucy teased, sliding down in the chair. "He's supposed to be real dumb."

"Dumb like a fox. It's like a game with him. He knows he's being watched, y'see. So he sets up little decoys and distractions. Took the boys a while to figure out he's got his lights on a timer. It looks for all the world like he's watching TV, then the downstairs lights go out and the bedroom light goes on for about fifteen minutes. Then it goes off. We thought he was sound asleep in bed till an off-duty cop spotted him at the pool hall in Gilead. And I'll tell you somethin', Lucy. The more I know about this guy, the creepier he gets."

"Really?" Lucy sat up straighter.

"Yeah. We tried searching his house, but it was pretty near impossible. He's got stuff piled up all around, and little pathways in between to get from room to room. He could have anything in there, buried under the boxes of newspapers and crap.

"And the kitchen. Lucy, I thought I'd seen dirty, but I was wrong. His was the worst I've ever seen." Barney's disgust came through the telephone line. "Except for his bathroom. I'm not sure he doesn't wash engines in his bathtub. Or keep pigs there. Gives the word filth new meaning."

"Couldn't the board of health condemn it or something?"

"Turned out they couldn't. DA said the ACLU'd be on it faster'n a tick on a dog. Individual rights, or some nonsense or other."

"Oh. What about Monica's rights?" Lucy was indignant. "The rights of the people whose property he burned."

"I guess the ACLU doesn't care about them. Don't worry, Lucy. We're keepin' an eye on him. Sooner or later he'll screw up. Lab says he's using alcohol to start the fires and it's a piss-poor accelerant. If it hadn't been so dry lately, the buildings wouldn't even 've burned. We'll get him. It's just a matter of time."

"I guess you're right. You know, Barney, every time I talk to you I get this nagging feeling that there's something I should tell you."

"About the kids?"

"No, that's not it. It'll come to me, but it's driving me crazy. I just haven't been the same since the baby. I keep forgetting things."

"I guess that's to be expected," said Barney indulgently. "You've got a lot on your mind. If you think of it, give me a call. Okay?"

"Yeah. Bye."

Lucy lifted the last sack of groceries from the cart and put it in the wayback, then slammed down the hatch. She returned the cart, then slipped Zoe out of the corduroy carrier and strapped her into the safety seat. Relieved to be unburdened, Zoe seemed to be gaining so fast, she slipped behind the wheel of the Subaru and turned the key in the ignition.

Checking the gas gauge, she decided to stop and fill the tank before going home. Lenk's Northstar, she remembered was just down the road.

Pulling into the rather ramshackle station, she wondered what the Northstar people saw in it. The paving was old and worn, the two pumps were dented, and the building needed paint. Of course, they planned to replace all that. But why this station? Did they really think Lenk would keep the new station up to their standards?

Not likely, she decided. Most probably they were using Lenk as a front man, while the project gathered the necessary permits and approvals. Local boards would find it harder to turn down one of their own, where they wouldn't hesitate to refuse a big corporation eager to cash in on the tourist economy. Once the project was approved, Lucy guessed, Northstar would buy out Randy Lenk. No wonder he got so mad at the hearing. He probably stood to gain a lot of money from this deal.

"Fill it up, please," said Lucy to the kid manning the pump. "Do you mind if I look around?" she asked, waving a hand at a pile of junk next to a shed. "I lost the cap to the tank on my snowblower. Maybe you've got one that'll do."

"Sure," said the kid with a shrug.

He looked up as Miss Tilley zoomed into the space on the other side of the pump, and rolled down the window of her huge Chrysler Imperial.

"Nice car," Lucy heard him say in an admiring voice as he went to wait on her.

She lifted Zoe out of the baby seat, and zipped her into the corduroy carrier she wore on her chest. Not quite sure what she hoped to find, Lucy began sifting through the pile. There were bits and pieces of all sorts of machinery, car parts, a snowplow, even a sewing machine. Just the sort of stuff that might come in handy, she thought wryly, especially if you were going to be very rich.

I wonder what he'll do with his money, she thought. Buy a big mansion and surround it with odds and ends in his best backwoods fashion. Maybe better grade car parts, she chuckled to herself. BMW hubcaps. Mercedes-Benz mufflers. Rhino guards from Range Rovers; also handy for moose.

Standing on tiptoe, she grasped the windowsill and tried to peek in. The window was filthy, and the sun was too bright. She couldn't make out a thing. The shed could be filled with cans of alcohol and she'd never know.

Why alcohol, when he had all this gas? she wondered. Why not? It was probably supposed to fool the cops. Just the sort of reasoning someone like Lenk would use.

"Whaddya think you're doin?"

Lucy jumped and wrapped her arms protectively around the baby. She turned slowly, reluctant to face Randy Lenk. His dirty hair fell into his eyes and he had a three-day stubble of beard. His teeth, she was appalled to see, really were green.

"What the hell do you think you're doin'?" he growled.

"By any chance," she said politely, "do you have a cap that would fit the gas tank of a Toro snowblower? I somehow lost mine."

"Nope." His voice was flat.

"Could I just take a peek in the shed?" persisted Lucy. "You've got so much stuff around here—I bet you've got something I could use. I'd be happy to pay for it."

Lenk narrowed his eyes and stepped closer. Lucy could smell his sour scent.

"If you know what's good for you, you'll get outta here," he snarled.

"Fine. No problem," said Lucy, stepping backward. Not too hasty, she told herself. Stay calm. Don't panic. Back to the car.

"How much do I owe you?" she asked the attendant once she reached her car.

"Ten," said the kid.

"Here you go. Thanks."

Lucy repeated the business of strapping Zoe into the car seat. Then she started the ignition and pulled up behind Miss Tilley, who was signaling to turn left.

That Chrysler certainly was some car, she thought, as she waited her turn to exit. Acres of solid black hood and trunk were trimmed with massive chrome grilles and heavy bumpers. There was no plastic on this baby. Everything was shining, gleaming metal. It was easily twice as big as her Subaru. What had Bill told her? It was the favorite model of demolition derby drivers.

"Those things are built like tanks," he'd said. "They just don't make 'em like that anymore."

Too bad, thought Lucy. That car had certainly given Miss Tilley good service. She'd had it forever. Of course, she had taken good care of it. There wasn't a speck of rust on it.

Sensing movement ahead, Lucy automatically flipped the signal stick, and shifted into first, ready to follow the Chrysler. Instead of accelerating gradually, however, Miss Tilley's Chrysler suddenly lurched ahead, apparently out of control.

Careening wildly into oncoming traffic, the huge black car smashed head on into a tiny red Toyota Tercel.

CHAPTER TWENTY-FIVE

The sickening thud of the collision was still echoing in Lucy's ears when she remembered what she had meant to tell Barney. She had wanted to discuss Miss Tilley's erratic driving, in hopes of avoiding an accident like the one she had just witnessed.

Fighting off shock and willing her wooden limbs to move, Lucy hurried up to Miss Tilley.

"Are you all right?" she demanded, yanking the door open.

"I seem to be," answered the old woman. Her voice was shaky and uncertain, and her eyes weren't quite focused.

Giving her hand, which was still clutching the steering wheel, a quick pat, Lucy rushed over to the red Tercel.

The damage was worse than she thought. The entire front hood had crumpled under the force of the impact, it was simply gone. The tiny naked wheels were askew; the windshield was smashed; the doors deeply dented.

"I can't get the door open," panted the gas station attendant. For the first time, Lucy noticed that the name embroidered on his shirt was Rob.

"Did somebody call rescue?"

"Yeah. The boss." He grunted, straining to wrestle the twisted metal open.

"I think they'll have to use the jaws of life or something," said Lucy. "Who's the driver?" Leaning forward she peered through the crackled side window.

"Oh, no." Her legs buckled under her in shock as she recognized the driver. She stumbled forward, catching herself on the tiny car. "That's Jennifer."

"Yeah. She don't look too good, either."

Jennifer was unconscious, her face cut and bleeding. But that wasn't what worried Lucy. With no airbag to protect her, Jennifer must have been thrown against the steering wheel, suffering internal injuries. The way the car folded in the crash, Lucy knew the weight of the engine would be crushing her legs and feet.

"When are they going to get here?" Lucy moaned, growing frantic at the delay.

"I hear a siren," said Rob.

Lenk appeared next to them, carrying a filthy old quilt. Lucy took it with shaking hands and went to help Miss Tilley out of her car.

"Help is on the way," said Lucy, swallowing hard to avoid sobbing. "Here, let me help you out of the car. We'll put this blanket around you and you can sit in my car."

Miss Tilley didn't respond, so Lucy took her elbow. Moving slowly and stiffly, she allowed Lucy to help her out of the big old Chrysler. As far as Lucy could see, except for a smashed headlight and a few dents, the car was undamaged.

"Who's in the other car?" asked Miss Tilley, as Lucy put the nasty quilt around her shoulders.

"Jennifer Mitchell."

"Is she all right?" Lucy felt Miss Tilley's hand tighten on her arm.

"I don't know. We can't get the door open."

Lucy got Miss Tilley settled in the passenger seat of the Subaru, then climbed in behind the wheel. She wanted to move the car out of the way, to give the arriving rescue workers plenty of room to work. Her hands trembled as she turned the ignition key; she wanted to drive away as fast as she could.

She couldn't do that. She had witnessed the accident; she had Miss Tilley in her car. She was sure they would have to answer some questions. She shifted the car into reverse and parked in the corner of the gas station.

Realizing that Zoe was fussing in her car seat, Lucy got out of the car. She unfastened the straps holding the baby and lifted her up, pressing her tiny body against her chest. Holding Zoe against her shoulder, and patting her back, Lucy paced back and forth alongside the passenger side of the car.

"I hope she isn't hurt," said Miss Tilley.

Not much chance of that, thought Lucy, drawing Zoe closer. She was supposed to be consoling the baby, but instead, she was drawing strength from Zoe's regular breathing and sweet warmth. Instinctively rubbing her chin against Zoe's fuzzy head, she tried to reassure Miss Tilley.

"She's in good hands."

They watched as the rescuers went about their work. An ambulance and a fire engine were on the scene, police cruisers had arrived and officers were directing traffic away from the wreck. Rescue workers, dressed in fire hats, slickers, and boots went back and forth between the vehicles and their truck, getting supplies and equipment. Lucy heard the whine of power machinery, and the ever-present cackle of the radios.

A fireman was pumping white foam out onto the road, and Lucy belatedly realized there was a chance of the whole mess exploding and going up in flames.

"Oh, God, please let Jennifer be okay," she whispered, closing her eyes as tears rolled down her face. "Please, please, please."

"I just have a few questions I need to ask you," said a young officer, approaching her.

Lucy brushed away her tears, and focused hard on his nameplate. "Kirwan, T." it read. He must be one of Dot Kirwan's boys, she thought, placing him. Dot Kirwan was a cheerful, gossipy lady who cashiered at Marzetti's IGA—several of her children worked in the police and fire departments.

"Did you witness the accident?" he asked, producing an accident report form.

Lucy nodded.

"Miss Tilley was driving the Chrysler?"

"Yes."

"Can you tell me what you saw?"

"All of a sudden her car started moving—fast," remembered Lucy.

"Do you think the brakes failed?"

"She didn't brake," said Lucy, picturing the rear end of the car. "The brake lights never went on." Lucy sniffled. "Is Jennifer going to be okay?"

For a moment, the young officer's true emotions broke through his professional demeanor, and Lucy caught a glimpse of ragged grief. He quickly caught himself, his back straightened, and he answered in clipped tones.

"They're doing everything they can, but I don't want to mislead you. It doesn't look good."

Lucy swayed a bit, catching herself against the Subaru.

"Can I take Miss Tilley home? She's very old. I'm worried she'll go into shock."

"Sure," he said. "Someone'll be in touch with you later."

After she had returned Zoe to her car seat and was back in the driver's seat, she turned to face Miss Tilley.

"I'm going to take you home."

"We mustn't leave."

"The officer said we could. They'll follow up later."

"I want to make sure Jennifer is all right. I remember when she got her first library card. Such a bright little girl."

"They'll soon have her out of the car and off to the hospital," Lucy lied. "Everything's going to be okay."

"Don't patronize me," snapped Miss Tilley. "Anyone can see she must be severely hurt. We must stay and make sure she's properly cared for."

"Trust me, they're doing everything they can," Lucy said, with a sudden flash of temper. Miss Tilley had been bossing people around for too long, she decided, starting the car. "We're in the way here."

Miss Tilley put up no further opposition as Lucy drove her home. By the time they arrived at her little half-Cape house, Lucy was beginning to regret her outburst. The poor old woman was doubtlessly carrying a heavy burden of guilt and grief, as well as the shock of the accident.

When Lucy helped her out of the car she noticed that her wrists stuck out of her coat sleeves like sticks, and she stood unsteadily for a minute until Lucy took her arm and helped her up the walk. She was probably living on nothing but tea and toast, guessed Lucy, as she went back for Zoe.

Lucy soon had Miss Tilley installed in her usual armchair, snugly wrapped in a soft afghan. Folding Lenk's filthy quilt, Lucy set it outside on the back porch. Returning to the kitchen, she sniffed. The house smelled stale, something she had never noticed before.

She put the kettle on to boil and looked for something for lunch. As she had guessed, the kitchen was poorly stocked. The refrigerator contained nothing but a stick of butter, a tube of hemorrhoid ointment, a bottle of lemon juice, and a bag full of flashlight batteries.

Shrugging, she turned to investigate the pantry, but found little there except a few cans of soup and vegetables. Standing on the floor, however, were quite a few empty sherry bottles. There was one on the shelf, half full, and she helped herself to a swig. Feeling its warmth spread through her, she took another.

Lucy popped the last four slices of bread in the toaster and dumped a can of cream of mushroom soup in a saucepan. She stirred in a bit of milk, and added some canned asparagus.

When she took the plates and cups out of the cabinet, she noticed that although they were neatly stacked, they were not very clean. Was it failing eyesight, she wondered, or too much sherry?

Lucy quickly washed the dishes and made a tray for Miss Tilley. Perching opposite her, with a plate balanced on her knees, Lucy quickly devoured her meal. She hadn't realized how hungry she was, or how tired. The morning's events had sapped her energy.

Zoe, also, was ready for lunch. Lucy picked her up and settled back in the couch to nurse and sip her tea.

Miss Tilley, she observed, was only playing with her food.

"You should try to eat."

"It's the speed," said the old woman, shaking her head. "These young people drive too fast."

"What do you mean?"

"If that young woman hadn't been driving so fast, I would have seen her."

Lucy sputtered in her teacup. "Are you saying the accident was Jennifer's fault?"

"Of course. It couldn't be my fault. I've been driving for seventy years, and I've never had an accident. I have a perfect driving record."

"What about my mailbox?" Lucy reminded her. "You knocked it right over. And Franny Small? You nearly smashed into her last week."

"Franny is notoriously absentminded. She shouldn't be allowed to drive."

"And my mailbox? Did it leap in front of you?"

"Well, it is in an awkward location . . ."

"Nonsense. It's precisely where it's supposed to be. And it's high time you stopped blaming everybody and everything for your own mistakes. You're too old to drive."

As soon as the words were out Lucy regretted them. Miss Tilley looked as if she'd been slapped in the face.

"I am not too old to drive. My father drove until the day he died. He was ninety-four."

And he probably died in one hell of a crash, thought Lucy, propping Zoe on her shoulder and burping her.

"Everyone is different. Don't forget the roads are busier now." Lucy laid Zoe down on the couch and began to change her diaper. "I think you should consider giving up your license. If you don't, after what's happened, I'm afraid they'll suspend it."

"Even though the accident wasn't my fault?"

"Enough," said Lucy, firmly snapping the diaper cover in place. "I saw everything. The accident was definitely your fault."

Miss Tilley poked at a piece of toast with her fork. Honestly, thought Lucy, she was as stubborn as a two-year-old.

Miss Tilley looked up. "If I surrender my license, I'll lose my independence."

"You could ride the Senior Shuttle," said Lucy, referring to a van service provided by the local Senior Council.

"With all those doddering fools and half-wits? And you can't go when you want. You have to make an appointment."

"Take a taxi, then."

"Think of the expense! Not to mention having Billy Smits knowing all my business."

"It's time to face facts. You need some help. To be honest, it seems to me you're not doing such a great job of housekeeping."

"Too busy." She waved a large, bony hand.

Lucy sat Zoe in her lap and held her tiny chest with one hand while she gently patted her back with the other.

"The house is dirty, you're not eating properly, you need to make some changes."

"Hmmph," said Miss Tilley, looking right past her head and out the window. "Look at handsome Mr. Bluejay, at the bird feeder."

Lucy turned and saw a bit of blue plastic bread wrapper caught on a twig.

"That's not," she began, but seeing the rapt expression on her old friend's face, she paused. "He is a handsome fellow, isn't he?"

CHAPTER TWENTY-SIX

Ted was just wrapping up an interview with Don Swazey, the owner of an impressive matchbook collection, when his pager went off. Glancing at the number, he asked permission to use the phone.

"It's me," he said to Phyllis, the imperturbable woman who answered the phone, took the classified ads, maintained the subscription list, and proofread all the copy.

"Oh, Ted, I think you better get over to Lenk's gas station. The scanner's been going crazy. Sounds like a bad accident."

"Damn," said Ted, who hated covering accidents. "I'm on my way," he said, and replaced the receiver. "Mr. Swazey, I'm afraid I've got to go. Do you mind if I take your picture for the paper?"

"Not at all. How about if I hold this one? It's the jewel in the crown of my collection," he said, proudly displaying an aged matchbook printed with palm trees.

"Fine," said Ted, raising the camera. "Now, where's that one from?"

"The Coconut Grove nightclub in Boston."

"You don't say," said Ted, reaching for the proferred bit of cardboard. Everybody knew about the tragic Coconut Grove fire; Ted had recently seen a piece about it in *New England Life* magazine, complete with photos of charred victims, still seated at their tables. The fire was thought to have started when some paper palm-frond decorations caught fire in the popular night spot that was packed with soldiers celebrating the end of World War II. The fire grew very quickly, consuming all the oxygen, so that those who hadn't burned to death had suffocated. Only a handful of the hundreds who packed the club that night had survived.

"I was one of the lucky ones," Mr. Swazey said.

"You were there the night of the fire?" Ted asked.

"Nope. The night before. We were going to go the night of the fire, but my date had to work. She was a nurse. So we moved it up. I proposed to her that night. Pretty lucky, hunh?"

"I'd say so," Ted agreed. "Thanks for the interview. I'm sorry I've got to run."

Fires, thought Ted. These days it always seemed to be fires. At least an auto accident would be a change, he thought, as he drove to the scene. A nice spectacular crash for page one. Something where the car was a total wreck, but the driver walked away without a scratch. That way he wouldn't have to call the grieving family for information about the deceased.

Some life this is, he muttered, as the cop directing traffic away from the accident waved him through. Maybe it was time to give up small-town news and go into public relations.

Approaching the little Tercel, Ted swallowed hard. This

looked like a bad one. Rescue workers had removed the roof of the little car, but were still unable to extricate the driver.

"Jeesus Christ," swore Fire Chief Pulaski. "Closest air bag's over at Wilton. Goddamn town meeting!" he exploded. Catching sight of Ted, he added, "And you can quote me on that!"

Ted nodded grimly, as the chief stormed past. Last spring Pulaski had asked town meeting voters to approve the purchase of a heavy-duty rescue air bag and they had turned him down. Now he had to borrow one from a neighboring town, losing precious time.

"Who's in the car?" he asked the kid who worked at the gas station.

"Jennifer Mitchell. The Medflight helicopter is on the way, but they can't get her out. Her legs are caught under the engine block."

Ted nodded. No wonder Pulaski was so upset. His daughter, Molly, played on the high school field hockey team with Jennifer. Ted usually covered the games, and had often seen Pulaski there, cheering the girls on. Ted remembered Jennifer running down the field in her regulation kilt, long blond hair streaming behind her, to score a goal.

That was the trouble with small towns, he remembered a state trooper telling him. You knew everybody—the crooks, the troublemakers, and the victims. He was sick of writing about the people he knew, his friends, and the horrible things that happened to them.

"Copter's landed on the football field," he heard a firefighter tell the chief.

"Damn," said Pulaski. "Where the hell is Wilton?"

"Out of my way, Stillings." Ted recognized Police Chief Crowley's gruff voice, and turned to face him. He was carrying a large aluminum case.

"Wilton broke down coupla miles from here," said Crowley. "Fella said you wanted this."

"Right," said Pulaski, reaching for the case. "C'mon, boys, let's get this thing under the engine."

As the men busied themselves positioning the airbag and starting the compressor, Ted began snapping pictures. He finished off one roll of film and reloaded, watching breathlessly as Pulaski gave the order and the airbag began to inflate.

At first, it seemed as if the weight of the engine block was too much for the bag; nothing moved. The compressor continued hissing and the bag grew larger and larger, until finally the crushed metal yielded, groaning in protest.

"Hold it there!" shouted Pulaski.

The fireman who was manning the compressor adjusted a valve, and the bag stopped growing. Ted held his breath; it seemed incredible that air pressure was powerful enough to lift the engine and keep it from crashing back down.

In a matter of seconds the medics had Jennifer out of the car and into the ambulance. Minutes later, Ted saw the helicopter rise into the sky and fly off toward the trauma unit at the hospital in Portland.

"That was pretty amazing," Ted said to Crowley.

"Nah," he answered. "Modern technology."

"Actually, I meant what you did. If you hadn't brought the airbag that girl would still be stuck in the car."

"It was nothin'," said Crowley. "I heard it on the radio, and happened to be in the vicinity."

"It's your day off," Ted persisted.

"What are you? Some kinda wise-ass, know-it-all reporter?"

Crowley's voice was just as gruff as ever, but Ted noticed a gleam of amusement in his eyes.

"You're damned right I am," he shot back. Ted gave him a quick salute and hurried back to his car. He had to get to the office. He had a story to write.

CHAPTER TWENTY-SEVEN

Leaving Miss Tilley's, Lucy also saw the Medflight helicopter, rising above the trees. She sent a little prayer along with it, as it banked and whirled off to the trauma center, the same prayer she had been repeating ever since the accident. Please, please God, let Jennifer be okay.

The poor girl must have been trapped in that car for at least an hour and a half, thought Lucy, as she started up the Subaru. That couldn't be good. Everything she knew about first aid stressed the fact that minutes could mean the difference between life and death. At least Jennifer had youth on her side, and was strong and healthy.

Miss Tilley, on the other hand, was old and weak, much weaker than anyone guessed. Now that she thought about it, Lucy could see a pattern of increasing intolerance. Miss Tilley had always been something of a character, but lately her tongue had been sharper and her wit more scathing. Lucy suspected this was her way of compensating for her increasing frailty.

The old woman had no family that Lucy knew of. Dear Poppa, as Miss Tilley always referred to her father, had died during the second Nixon administration. Miss Tilley always maintained that the shock of learning a Republican could be involved in something as disgraceful as Watergate had killed him.

With no family to take charge, Lucy knew she would have to assume the burden of making sure her old friend got the help she needed. There wasn't anybody else. Lucy decided to call the Senior Council as soon as possible to find out what resources were available.

Stopping at the traffic light on Main Street, Lucy spotted Toby and his constant companions, Eddie Culpepper, Adam Stillings, and Rickie Goodman. Stubby Phipps was trailing along after them, and if he didn't quite seem to be part of their group, they were tolerating him. Barney's social rehabilitation program seemed to be working.

They were probably headed to the scene of the accident, in hopes that the wrecked automobiles hadn't been towed away yet. She wondered if she should stop them. She could order them into the car and take them home, get out some board games, and cook up some popcorn in the microwave.

No, she thought. They might as well see. Maybe they would remember when they were driving themselves. Not, she thought with a sigh of relief, for at least a few more years.

Driving down Main Street, she passed the movie theater that had burned in July. The facade was boarded up with plywood, but the marquee bravely proclaimed the upcoming opening of an art exhibit.

COMING SOON it read in big black letters. COLLEGE ARTS COMPLEX. Smaller letters were arranged in the bottom row. "Premier show: The Red Zone."

A bit further along the road, Lucy saw the ruins of Doug Durning's real estate office. Like the Homestead, it had burned completely. Looking at the pile of charred timbers that remained, surrounded by official yellow tape, Lucy felt sick. It had been a beautiful old building, a real treasure, and now it was gone. What a shame. If this kept up the town wouldn't have any old buildings left.

"Oh my God," she said aloud, remembering the groceries in the wayback. At least there was no ice cream, she thought, grateful for small favors and crisp fall temperatures. Everything was probably fine.

By the time she got home she was so tired she was tempted to leave the groceries in the car for Bill to unload. Zoe didn't wake, however, when she lifted her out of the safety seat, so she decided she might as well get it done.

She was putting two boxes of instant oatmeal in the pantry, a buy one-get one-free special, when the phone rang.

"Lucy, it's Mira."

"Oh, hi," said Lucy. "How's everything?"

"Okay, I guess. I take one day at a time." Mira's voice sounded small.

"That's all you can do," said Lucy sympathetically.

"I wanted to let you know about the memorial service we've planned for Mom. It's Sunday, at First Parish here in Brookline. Two o'clock."

"Thanks for calling," said Lucy. "We'll be there."

But when she hung up, Lucy realized she didn't want to spend an hour thinking about poor Monica, burned to cinders in her bed.

She didn't want to think about Jennifer, fighting for her life in a Portland hospital. And she didn't want to think about Miss Tilley, slowly decomposing in her musty, dusty old house.

Up until now, she thought, she'd been concerned with conceiving and planting and growing. That was her job—tending the garden, keeping the house, and raising the children. She had nothing to do with death. Even her father's sudden passing from a heart attack hadn't really touched her. She'd been so busy taking care of the details and helping her mother that she had barely noticed her loss.

But now, more than anything, she missed her father. She wished he could come back and sit in his favorite spot at her kitchen table. She remembered him there on Sunday mornings, with a mug of coffee and a cigarette, tackling the *Times* crossword puzzle.

He was gone. Sometimes she thought she saw him, an old guy in a plaid shirt jac and a tweed driving cap; sometimes she got a whiff of wool and cigarettes that reminded her so strongly of him, but it never was.

She brushed away a tear, feeling suddenly much older, and she knew she had crossed some invisible line. She heard a late autumn bluebottle fly buzzing at the window, and watched as it faltered, searching for an exit. There was only one way out—for the fly, for her, and even for baby Zoe.

CHAPTER TWENTY-EIGHT

Promptly at ten on Halloween Lucy met Liz Kelly, the outreach worker from Senior Services in front of Miss Tilley's house. Liz was much heavier than Lucy expected, but she had given Lucy reason to be optimistic during their brief phone conversation the day before.

Liz hadn't hesitated to schedule an outreach meeting for Saturday morning. After hearing Lucy describe Miss Tilley's situation she had agreed it required immediate action.

Today, however, Lucy was having doubts. As she watched Liz square her shoulders and march up to the front door, for all the world like a soldier going into battle, she wished she were certain this was the right thing to do.

"Good news," chirped Miss Tilley, as she opened the door. "The man from the auto body shop called and said my car will be just fine. There was no mechanical damage. He says it will be good as new once he pops out a few dents and slaps on some paint. His choice of words, not mine."

Lucy felt a small bubble of anger welling up in her throat, and she swallowed it down. Scolding at the old woman wouldn't accomplish anything. It certainly wouldn't help Jennifer.

"That's all well and good then," said Liz, carefully lowering her rather ample bottom onto Miss Tilley's prize Windsor chair. It squeaked a bit, but held, much to Lucy's amazement. She had expected the chair to splinter under Liz's weight. "You'll be able to get a good price when you sell it."

"I don't plan to sell it," said Miss Tilley.

"Of course you're going to sell it," said Liz, with all the subtlety of a bulldozer. "You can't continue to drive after what happened."

"I certainly can. If I stop driving I'll lose my independence. It would be like giving up and dying."

"That's ridiculous," said Liz flatly. "Besides, they'll probably revoke or suspend your license. You'll be lucky if you don't go to jail. I heard the police are considering manslaughter charges, maybe even vehicular homicide, if Jennifer dies."

"Is that true?" Miss Tilley turned to Lucy. "Is she going to die?"

"I don't know," Lucy answered. "I called the hospital this morning and they said she was in intensive care. She's listed in poor condition."

"Well, there's no use crossing that bridge until we get to it," said Liz brightly. "And if the need arises, Senior Services has free legal counseling. In fact, I think you'll be amazed at the range of services we offer. I like to tell people it's like an all you can eat buffet. You take all the services you want and leave the rest."

Lucy doubted Miss Tilley had ever attended an all you can eat buffet; in fact, she suspected her old friend would find the very idea repulsive.

"I think I'll put the kettle on," said Lucy, rising. As she puttered about in the kitchen, she listened to the conversation in the other room.

"We have Meals on Wheels," said Liz. "Delicious hot nutritious meals brought right to your home every day."

"Macaroni and cheese in tin foil," snorted Miss Tilley.

"We have trained home care aides, to help you with light housekeeping and personal care."

"Snoops and busybodies." Miss Tilley waved away the brochure.

"We have friendly visitors, volunteers who will pay you a visit to brighten your day."

"Ghouls," Miss Tilley snapped. "Waiting to snatch the silver."

"What shall I put you down for?" asked Liz, licking her pencil.

"You can get lead poisoning doing that," said Miss Tilley. "Not to mention that it's a very unattractive habit." She folded her hands in her lap.

"Maybe you'd like to think about it for a bit," Lucy suggested, bringing in the tea tray. "She doesn't have to decide today, does she?"

"Oh, no," Liz agreed. "Give me a call anytime. Actually," she checked her watch, "I have to scoot, or I'll be late for a meeting."

"Don't let me keep you," said Miss Tilley.

"I can see what you meant when you called yesterday," Liz whispered as Lucy showed her to the door. "She's a stubborn old dear, but she'll come around. They all do. They fight it at first, but eventually they realize that they need help."

"We'll work something out," said Lucy. "Thanks for coming." Standing in the tiny hall with Liz, Lucy felt smothered.

"Some of these old folks live in shocking conditions, but this is the worst I've seen in a while." Liz raised an eyebrow. "Not even a TV."

"Oh, that's because . . ."

"I'm sure we can find her a used one. And that furniture! Absolutely filthy. Needs a good scrubbing if you ask me."

"Maybe a bit of lemon oil," said Lucy, imagining Liz taking a sudsy sponge to Miss Tilley's priceless antiques.

"Don't you worry, we'll soon have everything ship-shape." Liz patted Lucy's hand and clumped down the path in her sensible shoes, clutching her flowing Guatemalan wrap around her bulky form.

"What a remarkably ugly woman," said Miss Tilley, when Lucy returned. "Why doesn't she get that huge hairy mole removed?"

"Beats me," said Lucy. She took a sip of tea. "Is it true that you don't cash your social security checks?"

"That's rather a personal question, don't you think?"

"I was thinking that if you cashed them you could hire someone to help out a couple of hours a day. Cook a hot meal for you, and drive you wherever you wanted to go."

"Like Cynthia Durning?"

"Who?" Lucy was distracted, today she didn't have the patience to listen to one of Miss Tilley's stories. She couldn't help worrying about Jennifer.

"Douglas's mother. She kept house for Wilfred Peters for years. Some people said she did more than keep house." The old woman cackled wickedly. "That's why old Peters left her his house. Too bad it's gone, now."

"It's too bad," Lucy repeated.

"That's right. Used to be Mr. Peters's house. People talked, of course, but I thought it was fitting, really. He didn't have any family except for that daughter of his who ran off with Rupert Lenk. After that Mr. Peters wouldn't have anything to do with her, and I think he was absolutely right. He warned her she was throwing her life away, that Lenk was trash. And he was."

"Who was Rupert? Randy's father?" Lucy snapped to attention. This was getting interesting.

"That's right. He was a vicious sort of man, and never took care of anything. He would have let it fall to rack and ruin, of course. When Randy was a little boy I wouldn't even let him in the library, he was so foul-mouthed and dirty. Just like his father. Douglas, on the other hand, was such a nice, polite boy. I felt badly when he brought that project of his before the commission and we had to turn him down. It didn't set well with a lot of people."

"What project? Do you mean Doug Durning's place?"

"That's right. The old Peters house." Miss Tilley was growing impatient. "He wanted to remodel that lovely old house into an office complex. It was quite grand, with a gazebo and an ATM machine. But it wasn't very well thought out. He was going to rip off that fine pine clapboard and stick in a stainless steel machine!"

"Really?" Lucy sighed. She couldn't spend all day sitting around with Miss Tilley. She had to get ready for the Halloween party tonight. Not that she felt like going to a party.

"It was one of the first cases that came before us," reminisced Miss Tilley. "In fact, he just missed the deadline. If he'd submitted his plans a day or two earlier, he wouldn't have needed commission review." Miss Tilley gave a big yawn. "I'm tired today. I didn't sleep very well last night."

"Why don't you take a little nap?" Lucy suggested, rising. "I'll clean up the tea things." She had to get moving, she had a million things to do.

Lucy took the tray into the kitchen and began filling the sink. The trash was full so she carried it outside to empty into the barrel that stood on the back porch. As she lifted the lid she noticed Lenk's quilt on the bench, where she'd left it the day before.

It always seemed to keep coming back to Lenk, she thought. What had Miss Tilley said? Doug Durning had inherited a house from Randy's grandfather. Was it his office? she wondered. Was that what it was all about? Had Randy been simmering with jealousy all these years, and finally decided to do something about it? Something spectacular that everybody would notice?

Lucy picked up the quilt and fingered it thoughtfully. It wouldn't hurt to stop off at Lenk's gas station to return the quilt. Maybe this time she would find a clue, something that would connect Lenk to the fires.

She went back inside and finished washing the tea things, leaving them to dry on the drainboard. Tiptoing, so as not to disturb Miss Tilley, she went into the front room to retrieve her purse.

"I'm not asleep," said the old woman.

"I have to go."

She nodded, and grasped Lucy's hand. "I've been thinking. I've decided to surrender my driver's license."

"I think that's the right thing to do."

"Did you notice that young man who works for Lenk?"

"Rob?"

"He seemed awfully taken with my car. I bet he'd enjoy driving it around town, even with me in it."

"That's a good idea."

"Who knows? If he really likes my classy chassis, I might even leave it to him."

"You're a filthy old witch," said Lucy fondly, placing her hand on Miss Tilley's shoulder and bending down to kiss the top of her grizzled head.

"I know," said Miss Tilley.

CHAPTER TWENTY-NINE

Lucy wished she had thought to put Lenk's quilt in a bag; it was so saturated with oil and grease that it left her hands feeling dirty.

Nothing the matter with a little dirt, she told herself, taking the quilt out of the car. You can always wash your hands.

She crossed the gritty asphalt of the service station and opened the office door.

"I'm returning your blanket," she said, cautiously poking her head in.

Lenk stared at her, his little piggy eyes were hostile.

"I'll just put it down here," said Lucy, abandoning her plan of looking for clues in her hurry to escape.

"Not so fast," he growled. "You're married to Stone, ain't ya?"

"I'm married to Bill Stone, if that's who you mean."

"That's the guy. I want you to tell him about this," said Lenk, waving a piece of limp letterhead in front of her face.

Lucy stepped forward, reaching for the letter, and heard the office door thud shut behind her. It was broad daylight, she was in a public place, so why did she feel trapped? Was it the confined space of the office, the clutter of papers and the stacks of dusty old cardboard boxes that climbed the walls?

"I'll tell him," said Lucy. "What is it?"

"That's for me to know and you to find out," teased Lenk, sensing her discomfort.

"I'm outta here," said Lucy, turning to go.

"There a fire or something?" he asked, putting a hand on the door and holding it shut. "It's from Northstar, that's what it is. They don't want my station anymore—they're not renewing my contract."

"Let me see that," said Lucy.

The letter was short and to the point. Following the meeting with the historical commission, Northstar's marketing department had reviewed the situation and determined that an alternative location would be preferable for their full-service station. In line with the company's current marketing policies, they would be unable to renew Mr. Lenk's contract as a dealer. They were grateful for Mr. Lenk's years of participation as a member of the Northstar team and wished him all the best in the future.

Lucy had a sinking feeling in the pit of her stomach. She slowly raised her eyes and met Lenk's.

"It's because of the commission. I lost my chance to fix up the station—'cause o' your husband!" He shoved his face right in hers, giving her the full benefit of his foul breath.

"It wasn't just Bill," said Lucy, standing her ground. "They didn't even vote. They asked Northstar to come back with an improved plan, that's all."

"Big companies like Northstar ain't gonna waste time on a bunch o' small-town cranks. They can go anywhere. They sure don't need me. They'll put whatever kinda station they want out on the highway—they'll put an igloo out there if they want."

"You're right," said Lucy, sympathizing with him in spite of herself. "Can't you become an independent dealer? Get some no-name gas?"

"Lookee here, missy," he said, pointing a blackened finger at her. "This here's all your fault, you and that husband o' yours. Think you can move in and tell people what to do. That commission wrecked the best deal I was ever gonna get."

Lenk was working up quite a head of steam and Lucy decided the office was definitely too small for both of them. The pungent smell of gasoline and assorted engine fluids, not to mention Lenk himself, was overpowering. Her head began to swim.

"Who's gonna make that up to me, hunh?" he demanded, stepping closer to her. "Nobody, that's who!" His face was just inches from hers. "I got screwed, and I know who did the screwing."

Lenk paused for breath, and Lucy took the opportunity to slip through the door. Her heart was pounding wildly as she gulped great mouthfuls of fresh air. Hurrying to the car, she quickly climbed inside, half expecting him to follow her. He didn't, however. In fact, when she looked back and saw him standing in the doorway, she could have sworn he was laughing at her.

CHAPTER THIRTY

"I don't like it one bit," Lucy complained to Bill. "He's really got a grudge against you, you know. I wouldn't be surprised if we came home tonight and found the house burned to a pile of cinders."

"Chief Crowley promised to put on an extra patrol—said he's aware of the situation and keeping an eye on things."

"Why doesn't that make me feel a whole lot better?"

"Do you want me to stay home? I could borrow a shotgun from Mr. Sanford." The Sanfords were the Stones' nearest neighbors on Red Top Road, and Mr. Sanford was always taking potshots at the groundhogs that raided his garden.

"And miss the party? We'll just have to hope for the best," Lucy grumbled, slipping the last of the dinner plates in the dishwasher and shutting the door. "Now, would you please get down those boxes on the top shelf."

"Sure. What's in them?"

"Cupcakes. Twelve dozen."

"When did you have time to bake cupcakes?"

"In batches. I got the last two dozen done this morning. Zoe didn't go back to sleep after her midnight snack so I baked cupcakes."

"In the middle of the night? You're nuts," said Bill.

"Who needs sleep, anyway?" Lucy said, yawning.

"I'll take everybody out tomorrow so you can have a nice long nap," said Bill, slipping his arms around her. "It's a promise."

"Really?" Lucy turned her face up to his.

"Yup." He bent down to kiss her.

"Mom, Elizabeth's hogging all the makeup!" Sara burst open the pantry door.

Startled, Lucy turned.

"Sara, you look great!" Sara was already in her costume, the pink tutu she'd worn in the ballet recital last spring.

"This turtleneck itches," she complained, scratching her neck.

"You'll need it, though. It's cold tonight," said Lucy. "And it really doesn't show too much."

Elizabeth, she saw, was seated at the kitchen table surrounded by every cosmetic Lucy owned.

"Mom, don't you have any eye shadow?" Elizabeth was also wearing her tutu, but she'd added a plaid flannel shirt and a pair of clunky black oxfords.

"Is that your costume?" asked Lucy.

"Yup. I'm a punk ballerina."

"That's kind of cute. Want me to pierce your nose for you?"

"That's not funny, Mom." Elizabeth's tone was withering. "What I really need is a tattoo."

"I think we've got some. The kind that wash off."

"Yeah. Right." Elizabeth was skeptical.

"In a cereal box." Lucy went back in the pantry and emerged triumphant with a huge box of crispy flakes. She dumped the contents into a bowl, plucked out the cellophane-wrapped sheet of tattoos, and then carefully poured the cereal back into the box.

"You have to eat this stuff up, you know."

"Thanks, Mom. I will," said Elizabeth, studying her face in the mirror she had propped up. "Where should I put it? On my cheek?"

"On your neck?"

"Neat. Say, Mom, what are you going as?"

"Myself."

"You've got to wear a costume!"

"That's right," agreed Bill. He had stuffed himself into Lucy's black maternity tights, added a yellow and black striped T-shirt, and topped off his ensemble with a bobbing antennae headband.

"What are you supposed to be?"

"A bumblebee. I thought it was obvious."

"I get it," said Lucy, stifling a giggle. "You just took me by surprise."

"I need a stinger. Got any ideas?"

"Aluminum foil?"

"Great." Bill ripped a big sheet off the roll, sat down, and began shaping it.

"Mom, I can't find one of my hairy hands," bellowed Toby from upstairs. "The left one."

"Did you look under your bed?"

"I can't find it anywhere," he insisted.

"I'd better help him," said Lucy. "Not too much makeup, okay, girls?"

"Sara, why don't you try this Very Berry lipstick," offered Elizabeth, in a rare display of sisterly helpfulness.

Lucy ran upstairs to Toby's room. As always, it was a mess, with clothes and books and athletic gear strewn everywhere. She sighed.

"Toby, it's no wonder you can never find anything. You have absolutely got to clean this room tomorrow."

"Oh, Mom," he groaned. "You should see Rickie's room. My room is neat compared to his."

"Right." Lucy didn't believe a word of it. She knelt down, lifted the dust ruffle, and peered under the bed. She reached in and shoved a few books aside. She pulled out the hairy hand glove.

"I looked, Mom. I swear."

"Oh, you looked all right. You just didn't move things around. Listen, I'm serious about this. Inspection is at fifteen hundred hours tomorrow, that's three o'clock. If you don't pass, you're grounded. This room is unhealthy. It's an accident waiting to happen. It's a fire hazard."

"So, how do I look?" Toby turned to face her. He resembled a very short Lon Chaney, in his werewolf mask and gloves, plaid shirt and jeans.

"Aaaah," screamed Lucy, running from the room and clattering downstairs. "Run for your lives! It's the wolf man!"

Bill and the girls looked up.

"Mom, where's your costume?" asked Elizabeth.

"I told you. I'm not wearing one."

"You'll have more fun if you do," coaxed Bill.

"I haven't given it any thought."

"You could be a fairy princess," offered Sara. "Or Wonder Woman."

"Or a witch," suggested Elizabeth.

Lucy rolled her eyes at Bill.

"I know," he suggested brightly. "I bet Toby's baseball uniform would fit you."

Lucy went back upstairs and pulled the uniform out of Toby's bottom drawer. She took it into her room and tried it on. Standing in front of the mirror, she decided she looked like a stuffed sausage. So much for all that exercise at the Body Shop.

Bill appeared behind her and wrapped his arms around her.

"This makes me look awfully busty," complained Lucy.

"I noticed," said Bill, nuzzling her neck. "You look great."

"I do?"

"Mmm," said Bill, turning her around to face him. They kissed, and Lucy felt something inside her stir that had been dormant for a long time. Bill led her to the bed.

"We can't do this," she protested. "The kids will come looking for us."

"The girls are so absorbed in making themselves up that they wouldn't notice an atom bomb. Toby's so scattered he never notices anything. Sometimes I worry about that boy," said Bill, pulling her down beside him.

"Mom, we're gonna be late," called Elizabeth. "What are you doing up there?"

"Your mother is putting on her costume, and I'm helping her. We'll be right down," said Bill. He grinned wickedly at Lucy.

"I've never done it with a bumblebee before," said Lucy.

"How was it?"

"Sweet, like honey," she said, hooking her bra and pulling the baseball jersey over her head.

Detouring to Toby's room she found a baseball cap and slapped it on her head backward. Then she scooped up Zoe, who had been sleeping in her bassinet, and carried her downstairs.

"Have we got any black greasepaint?" she asked.

"Here," said Elizabeth, passing her a tube. Lucy bent down to see her face in the mirror, and drew a line across each cheekbone, under her eyes.

"Hey, Mom, you look pretty good," said Elizabeth. "Want some lipstick?"

"Okay."

"We've got Mostly Melon, Misty Mauve, Very Berry, and Great Grape."

"How about Misty Melon Mauve, or whatever."

"Great Grape is good. It's not as dark as it looks."

"Okay," said Lucy, smearing some on. She eased Zoe into the baby carrier and fastened the straps. "Have we got everything?" she asked, grabbing the diaper bag. "Everybody take a box of cupcakes. Don't drop them. Don't eat them," she added, as an afterthought.

As the family straggled out and headed for the car, Lucy set a bowl of candy out on the porch and dropped a lit flashlight into the jack-o'-lantern.

"That's in case there are any trick or treaters," she said, hopping into the passenger side front seat.

"Don't sit on your stinger," she cautioned Bill.

He carefully folded his shirt up, tucking the foil stinger against the small of his back, and slid behind the wheel.

"Have we got everything?" he asked. "Cupcakes?"

"I think we're all set," said Lucy, patting Zoe who was nuzzled against her chest. She glanced at the house. She had left the kitchen light burning, and the porch light. The jack-o'-lantern glowed, grinning a holiday welcome.

She thought of all the treasures the house contained. Her grandmother's silver. Old family photographs. Love letters from

Bill. The kids' report cards. If it burned, all those things would be lost.

She couldn't bear to think about it. Tonight she wasn't going to worry about fires or death or car accidents. Tonight she was going to have fun.

CHAPTER THIRTY-ONE

L ight was pouring from the windows of the old Hallett House when they pulled up under the porte cochère, and music could be heard from within. Night concealed the cracked clapboards and peeling paint—this was probably how the mansion had looked to guests arriving a hundred years ago.

"I'll let you out here," said Bill. "Looks like I'm going to have to park the car out in the field." He waited while Lucy and the kids scrambled out. When all was clear, Lucy gave him a little wave. "See you later," he said, as he slipped the Subaru into gear and drove off.

Climbing the steps, and approaching the heavy oak double doors, Lucy savored the moment. Maybe she was dressed in a ridiculous baseball costume, but she felt for all the world like a rich lady arriving at a magnificent mansion.

Entering the foyer, she paused. Black and orange streamers

hung from the ceiling, artificial spiderwebs adorned the doors and windows. The room was packed with people, in all sorts of costumes, and at first Lucy didn't recognize anybody.

"Hi, guys, let me take those cupcakes," said a woman dressed exactly like Morticia Addams.

"Sue, I didn't recognize you!" Lucy exclaimed. "You look fabulous. Is that a wig?"

"One hundred percent polyester," said Sue, fingering her long, wavy black locks. "It's machine washable—if you believe labels. You look pretty cute, yourself."

"Cute's a curse," muttered Lucy. "I've finally got boobs, but nobody ever gets to see them. The baby carrier covers them up."

"Refreshments are in here," said Sue, indicating the way with a tilt of her head.

Lucy followed Sue and her trailing bits of costume. Together they arranged the cupcakes at the end of a long table covered with an orange cloth.

"This is terrific," said Lucy, surveying the table laden with food, the decorations, and the crowd of happy faces. "You did a great job."

"It all came together, didn't it?" Sue smiled proudly.

"Look, that's Marge Culpepper." She indicated a large woman in a witch costume.

"And that's Barney, dressed in a prison uniform. Pretty clever."

"There's Rachel Goodman—quite the femme fatale."

"Wow," agreed Sue. Rachel, Rickie's Mom, was wearing a sensational movie star dress made of clingy gold lamé, which she had topped with a wavy blond wig and a pair of oversized sunglasses.

"Hi, guys," she said, hurrying over. "This seemed like a good idea but my underwire bra is killing me—I'd forgotten what a girdle feels like, not to mention high heels. I'm in agony."

"Well, you look mahvelous." Lucy turned to Sue. "Doesn't she?"

"Absolutely mahvelous. Want a cupcake?"

"Couldn't. Can't even breathe."

Three high school girls Lucy recognized as friends of Jennifer Mitchell's tottered over—they were wearing platform shoes from the seventies, miniskirts, crocheted vests, floppy hats, and granny glasses.

"How do we look? Did we get it right?" asked Biz Henderson.

"Disco . . . that was before our time, wasn't it?" Sue was all innocence.

"Definitely," agreed Lucy. "I, myself, was only a babe in arms. But from the little I remember, I'd say you look great."

"Thanks." The girls all smiled. "We're so happy tonight," continued Biz. "Did you hear? Jen is out of intensive care. Her mom says she's gonna be okay."

"That's great news," said Lucy. "When will she be coming home?"

"Not for a while. She has to have lots of rehab and stuff, but she isn't going to die or anything," said Biz.

Lucy pasted on a smile and tried not to think of the accident; how afraid she'd been that Jennifer wouldn't survive.

"We're going to visit tomorrow," added one of the other girls.

"Meanwhile, we're supposed to keep an eye on Jeff Ryan for her. He's her boyfriend and we don't want anybody else to grab him while she's in the hospital."

"You'd better get busy," said Sue. "Isn't that him, dancing with Laurie Frye?" Laurie was notorious.

"Do you believe her? Jen's in the hospital," muttered Biz, as the girls hurried off.

"Aren't you glad you're not sixteen?" asked Sue.

"No," confessed Lucy. "I think I'll circulate, and see what the kids are up to."

Strolling into the ballroom, where the games were set up, Lucy spotted Toby in the group clustered around the apple-bobbing tank.

The girls, she guessed, would not be interested in getting their faces wet and messing up their makeup. Sure enough, she soon found Sara engaged in a lively game of Duck, Duck, Goose. Elizabeth was standing in a corner, preening and gossiping with her friends.

Noticing that Zoe was becoming increasingly restless in the baby carrier, Lucy looked for a quiet corner. She found it in the drawing room, where tables and chairs had been placed. A coffee urn sat in the corner, surrounded by a tempting assortment of snacks donated by Tammy Kurtz at the Greengage Cafe.

Lucy poured herself a cup of hazelnut coffee, put a few of the chocolate-pecan treats on a paper plate, and headed for a shadowy corner. There she could enjoy her snack, and nobody would notice if she nursed Zoe, too. She slid the diaper bag under a chair and sat down.

A sense of well-being crept over her as Zoe began to suck and her milk let down. She smiled to herself and gently stroked the baby's plump little cheek. She took a sip of coffee, and followed it with a bite of cookie. It was delicious, and she tried to guess what the ingredients were. There was a shortcake base, a layer of nuts and caramel, and the whole thing was topped with a drizzle of dark chocolate. Without exact proportions, it would be hard to duplicate, she decided.

"Let's sit over here," she heard Doug Durning say, and looked up. She wouldn't have recognized him—he was dressed in black tie and tails, had slicked his hair back, and was wearing vampire teeth.

"Excuse me," he said to his companion, as he slipped the teeth into a white handkerchief. "That's better."

He was with Krissy, of all people. Well, she wasn't wasting much time, thought Lucy. Krissy was dressed in flowing white draperies that showed off her figure, and had frosted her hair. Lucy had no idea what her costume was. A fairy of some sort? A Midsummer Night's Dream? Maybe an early frost, she guessed, spotting some blackened leaves pinned to her shoulder.

"I just love this house," said Krissy, giving Doug a flirtatious smile.

Oh, ho, thought Lucy. Krissy must have given up on Dr. Mayes and was looking for somebody new. No doubt about it, Doug was attractive and he could stand a little attention. He'd been through a lot lately, with the fire and all.

"It would be such fun to fix it up. I'd use black and white in the foyer—keep it formal. But I'd go wild with color in the rest of the rooms. Red for the dining room, pink and gold for the ballroom—can't you just see it?"

"Sure," said Doug, popping a cheese puff into his mouth. "Sounds great. It would take a hell of a lot of cash, though."

"I suppose it would," said Krissy, drawing her finger around the rim of her coffee cup, and lifting her eyes to meet Doug's.

This is so funny, thought Lucy, stifling a giggle. The woman was clearly signaling her availability. She wished she could see Doug's reaction but his back was to her.

"This old building is in pretty bad shape," said Doug, eager to display his expertise. "The sills are probably rotted—there's a lot of water damage. The land is probably worth more without the house than with it."

"How can that be?" asked Krissy, slipping her finger in her mouth and sucking it.

Did I ever stoop to tricks like that? wondered Lucy. She and Bill had been together for such a long time that she really couldn't remember what it had been like to be single and seeking a mate.

"Because of the hysterical district, that's how. Anybody buying this land with the house would have to pour a ton of money into restoring it. If the house was gone, you could put anything you wanted here. It's a prime location, with a water view. Somebody'd snap it up, believe me."

"Business is way over my head," confessed Krissy, making her eyes very large. "I can't even balance my checking account."

Lucy almost snorted in disbelief. If the Body Shop's success was any indication, Krissy was an extremely shrewd business-woman.

"Say," said Doug, with studied casualness. "Whaddya say we split? Find someplace that serves something a bit stronger than coffee?"

"Sounds good to me," said Krissy, rewarding him with a sexy smile.

"So here you are," said Bill, joining Lucy at the table. "I've been looking for you everywhere. Having a good time?"

"I sure am," said Lucy, grinning. "I've been people watching. I just saw true love, or maybe it was true lust, bloom."

"Yeah?" said Bill, leaning across the table. "What happened?"

"Well, first she went like this," said Lucy, running her finger around the cup. "And then she did this." She put her finger in her mouth.

"That's pretty good," said Bill. "I'm interested. Wanna dance?

"With the baby?"

"Sure."

"So, you like kids?" said Lucy, leading the way to the dance floor.

CHAPTER THIRTY-TWO

A few days after Lucy had given birth to Zoe, a sock hop had taken place at the elementary school. Lucy hadn't gone, of course, but she'd heard nothing but raves about the dance, and the terrific deejay, Sammy Witherspoon.

Sammy was spinning the platters again, tonight, and Lucy could understand why the dance had been such a success. He chose classic rock songs that everybody knew, and that were appropriate for the whole family.

Lucy was having a grand time, and so was everybody else. They did the bunny hop and the electric slide, everybody sang along to the Beatles' "Yellow Submarine." Sammy pulled out funny old songs Lucy hadn't heard in years, like "Yellow Polka Dot Bikini" and the one about putting chewing gum on the bedpost overnight.

Age didn't seem to matter. Biz Henderson and her friends were dancing, so was Dotty Cooper, along with her grandson, Billy.

Everybody was smiling, their faces shiny with perspiration and their eyes sparkling under the mirrored disco ball.

"Everybody having a good time?" asked Sammy.

"Yes!" the crowd shouted back.

Lucy took Bill's hand and made her way to the wall, so she could rest her back. Zoe seemed to be getting heavier in the baby carrier as the evening went on.

"Great! There's gonna be more music later, but right now I've been asked to announce the winners of the costume contest. May I have the envelope, please?"

Sue scurried forward and presented Sammy with a crumpled piece of paper. He raised his eyebrows.

"Our accountants at the firm of Price and Pimplemousse do *not* vouch for the accuracy of these results," he said, smoothing out the paper. Everybody laughed.

"In the preschool category, the winner is . . . drumroll please . . . Emily Ford!"

Propelled by a push from her mother, Emily stepped forward to receive her trophy. She was dressed in a beautiful Cinderella costume. Lucy had heard it was a joint effort by Emily's mother and her grandmother, and that they had worked on it for weeks. Noting the shining hand-sewn beads and ribbon trim, Lucy didn't doubt it.

Sammy presented Emily, who was a bit overwhelmed by the crowd, with her trophy. She clutched it to her chest and ran back to her mother, earning a round of applause.

"Next, is the elementary school category. I've been told the judges had a particularly tough time deciding," said Sammy. "They were able to come to a decision, however, and the winner is . . . Jared Kirwan."

Jared raised his hands above his head in a victory sign and

dashed forward, throwing in a karate kick for good measure. He was dressed in a bright blue Mighty Morphin Power Ranger suit, and was clearly living the role. He grinned boldly when he received his trophy, revealing a mouth full of mostly missing teeth. The kid was an imp, a real crowd pleaser, and everyone clapped for him, including his grandmother, Dot.

Recalling Dot Kirwan's excellent connections, her son was a police officer and her daughter was the dispatcher at the fire department, Lucy sidled over to her.

"What a cute kid," she said.

"Oh, Jared's a handful. I don't know how you youngsters manage. This must be the new baby," she cooed, slipping her finger inside Zoe's clenched fist.

"She's been awfully good tonight, but I have to confess my back is killing me," Lucy said with a sigh.

"Those baby carriers are great, though. I wish we'd had them," said Dot.

"I don't know what I'd do without it," agreed Lucy. "Listen, Dot, what do you think about all these fires? Have you heard anything?"

"Actually," said Dot, leaning closer, "I think they're close to solving the case."

"Really? That would be such a relief. I've been so worried, especially since Doug's place burned. You know all the members of the commission got threatening phone calls?"

"Well, I don't want to mention any names," she nodded knowingly, "but I don't think you have to worry anymore."

Lucy was about to answer when she heard Stubby's name called.

Kicking the floor bashfully with his toe, Stubby stepped forward. He was dressed in one of Barney's old uniforms, cut down to size, Lucy guessed, by Marge. His heavy utility belt was complete with genuine handcuffs, a toy pistol, and a walkie-talkie.

"This prize is for the most authentic costume," said Sammy. "Say, Officer, don't arrest me, okay?"

"You're under arrest!" yelled Stubby, reaching for the handcuffs.

"Whoa," said Sammy. "If you handcuff me I won't be able to give you your prize."

He presented Stubby with a handsome trophy, and raised his hands over his head. "I give up, Officer," said Sammy. "Please, don't shoot."

Stubby pulled out his gun, waved it, and returned to the little gang of boys. They clustered around him, examing his prize. Lucy was smiling her approval when she heard Bill's name called.

"This prize is for the adult who absolutely does not care how ridiculous he looks, and I think you'll all agree that Bill Stone took a bit of a fashion risk tonight," said Sammy.

Everyone laughed as Bill stepped forward.

"Man, you are one ugly bumblebee," said Sammy. "I'd sure hate to meet you in the flower garden."

"You don't have to worry. My buzz is a lot worse than my sting," said Bill, turning to model his aluminum foil stinger.

Everybody clapped and cheered as he accepted his trophy, and gave the crowd a wave.

"Well, that concludes this portion of the program," said Sammy. "Let's party!" He flipped a switch, and the performer who used to be called Prince began encouraging everyone to "Party like it's 1999."

"Shall we dance?" asked Bill.

"I'm bushed," said Lucy. "I'd like to go home."

"Okay," he said. "You find the kids and I'll get the coats. Meet you in the foyer."

Lucy beckoned to Elizabeth and Sara, and led them to the hall, where they met Toby, along with Eddie, Richie, Adam, and Stubby.

"Toby, it's time to go."

"Aw, Mom, I don't wanna go home yet."

"It's late, and I'm too tired to argue . . ."

"It's not late," replied Toby. "It's not even nine o'clock."

"Don't talk back to me. It's time to go." Lucy was exhausted and she was in no mood for a discussion. "Get a move on," she snapped, not caring that she was embarrassing Toby in front of his friends.

"Leaving already?" asked Barney.

"I'm trying," said Lucy.

"That's a shame," said Barney. "The party's not over, and I promised the boys I'd take them trick-or-treating for a bit."

"Oh, I don't know," said Lucy, sensing that the battle had turned and she was losing.

"What's up?" asked Bill, materializing with his arms full of coats and jackets.

"Toby wants to stay and go trick-or-treating with the boys," explained Lucy. "What do you think?"

"No problem," said Bill. "Be home by ten at the latest, okay?"

"Sure, Dad," said Toby. "I promise."

"Relax, Lucy," said Barney. "I'll keep an eye on them. They won't get into any trouble."

"Okay," said Lucy, with a sigh of resignation. She'd heard that line before, last year, when the boys decorated the middle school principal's hedge with toilet paper. Toby had narrowly escaped suspension; he was lucky to get off with two weeks of after-school detention.

"I thought the whole point of this party was to keep kids off the streets," complained Lucy to Bill as they strolled down the hill to the car. "That way, they could have a safe Halloween, and have fun, too. And parents wouldn't have to go out of their minds worrying."

"Lucy, he'll be fine," said Bill, opening the car door.

"I'd feel a lot better if he was coming home with us," said Lucy, climbing in.

"Girls, what did you think of the party?" asked Bill, starting the engine.

"It was fun," said Sara.

"I don't see why Toby gets to stay and I have to go home," complained Elizabeth.

"I don't either," said Lucy, in rare agreement with her daughter. "It's too bad the weather's been so dry. If we'd had rain tonight, the boys wouldn't be able to stay out."

"Lucy, stop being a spoil-sport. You can't keep him tied to your apron strings forever. A boy's got to have some freedom. What's the world coming to if a kid can't have a few adventures on Halloween?"

"I guess you're right," Lucy said, thinking that she would feel a whole lot better if Toby was coming home with the rest of the family.

Looking out the car window as they drove along, Lucy noticed shadowy figures flitting from door to door. Passing one house, she saw a group of costumed children gathered on a brightly lit porch, where the festive decorations promised a generous welcome. Little white ghosts dangled from the porch roof, and a string of glowing pumpkin lights had been wrapped around the railing.

Cornstalks stood on either side of the door, sporting cheerful orange ribbons. A stuffed scarecrow lounged on the porch swing. The door opened and the group surged forward, eager to receive the treats a plump, grandmotherly woman was distributing. It could have been a scene from a Norman Rockwell painting.

She couldn't help smiling. Trick-or-treating was lots of fun, and where could it be safer than in a small New England town like Tinker's Cove?

CHAPTER THIRTY-THREE

When they got home, Lucy took baby Zoe upstairs and laid her down in the center of the big bed, still zipped in the corduroy baby carrier. She was sleeping soundly and Lucy didn't want to risk waking her.

She bent over the bed, arranging the baby, then straightened up. Arching her back and stretching, she tried to work out the kinks. Her back ached from wearing the baby carrier for such a long time.

"Did you have a good time, girls?" she asked, poking her head in the bathroom. Sara and Elizabeth were washing their faces.

"I would have had a better time if you didn't make me come home early," whined Elizabeth. "Toby gets to do whatever he wants. It's not fair."

"Life's not fair," said Lucy, picking up a brush and combing out her oldest daughter's hair.

"I don't see why Jared Kirwan won for his costume," fumed Elizabeth. "It was store bought. Mine was more original."

"What about you, pumpkin," said Lucy, turning to Sara. "Did you have a good time?"

"Daddy was funny," she said with a big smile. Her face was bright pink from the energetic scrubbing she'd given it. "I liked when he got the prize."

"Yeah, that was okay," Elizabeth agreed.

"Into your pajamas," Lucy urged, shooing them out so she could take possession of the bathroom. "I'll be in to kiss you good night."

She pulled off the baseball cap and shook out her hair. Then she washed her face with cool water. She hoped the baby would sleep well tonight, she could really use a good night's sleep. Tomorrow would be a long day—they were planning to attend the memorial service for Monica in Brookline. If there was time, she thought, maybe they could stop in at the hospital on the way home and visit Jennifer.

The girls were already in bed when Lucy went in to them. Elizabeth was reading Roald Dahl's *Witches*, but she put it down and climbed in bed with Sara when Lucy opened up Tasha Tudor's *Pumpkin Moonshines*. Both girls listened raptly as Lucy read the the story of a little girl's adventures with a huge jack-o'-lantern.

"I wish I could have a dress and bonnet like Sylvie," sighed Sara, pointing to one of the charming illustrations of Sylvie in her old-fashioned clothes.

"I wish I could paint my fingernails black," said Elizabeth.

"Time to go to sleep," said Lucy, closing the tiny book. She leaned over and kissed Sara on the top of her head. Sara reached up and wrapped her arms around her in a tight hug. Lucy squeezed back, glad that Sara was still a little girl who loved to hug her mommy. "Nighty-night," she said, tucking the covers around her. "Sleep tight."

"Can I read for a while?" asked Elizabeth, who had returned to her own bed.

"It's past your bedtime."

"It's Saturday. I don't have school tomorrow."

"It will disturb your sister."

"I'll use a flashlight."

"Okay," Lucy said, reaching down and caressing her cheek. "Not too late, now," she said, giving her oldest daughter a quick peck on the cheek. "Good night." She turned out the light.

Closing the girls' door, Lucy leaned against it for a minute. The party had thrown off her usual evening routine, and she wasn't quite sure what to do. Zoe was still sleeping soundly and she hated to disturb her. On the other hand, if she changed her diaper and nursed her now she might sleep through the night.

She was still weighing the decision when a whimper from the bedroom made it for her. She went into the nursery to get a diaper but discovered the basket was empty. With all the baking and planning for the party she had gotten behind in the laundry. She would have to get a disposable from the diaper bag.

Where had she left it? It wasn't on the kitchen chair where she usually dropped it. Was it in the car? With a flash of clarity she remembered shoving it under her chair when she had coffee at the party. It was probably still there.

"Bill, I left the diaper bag . . ." she began, intending to ask him to retrieve it for her. But Bill was sound asleep in his recliner, the zoning bylaws still in his hand.

"I might as well go get it myself," she decided, checking the baby who had settled back into a deep sleep. "I can be back in ten minutes," she said to herself, throwing on a jacket and grabbing the car keys.

CHAPTER THIRTY-FOUR

The Hallett House was dark and empty when Lucy arrived; it was the very image of a haunted house. She found this a bit disconcerting. She had expected to meet a few lingering party-goers, or at least the cleanup crew. Maybe even Toby and his band of trick-or-treaters.

She checked the dashboard clock and saw it was later than she thought, past ten o'clock. That explained it, she reasoned. Those with kids had taken them home to bed, and the serious party types had gone on to the scattered nightspots in the area that featured local bands and cheap drinks.

She hesitated, figuring the old house was probably locked up tight. Besides, the huge hulk of a mansion was not inviting as it loomed above her. This is too spooky, she thought, deciding to pick up a box of disposables at the Quik Stop.

Don't be ridiculous, she argued with herself, reaching for the flashlight she kept in the car. It was worth a try. Going to the Quik Stop would take at least twenty minutes more, and she was afraid Zoe might wake up.

As she climbed out of the car the full moon suddenly appeared from behind a cloud and the hill was flooded with light.

A good omen, she thought, as she hauled herself up the steps to the big front door and reached for the knob. To her surprise, it turned.

Lucy smiled. Thanks to someone's carelessness she would be able to grab the diaper bag and return home before she was missed.

Inside, the foyer was pitch black. Moonlight could hardly penetrate where bright sunlight never reached, blocked by the dilapidated porch and gloomy stained-glass windows. Lucy switched on the flashlight and cast the beam around the room. The floor was littered with discarded cups, and crepe paper streamers dropped from the ceiling. Sue must have decided to put off the cleanup until tomorrow.

Lucy heard a scuttling noise from one of the rooms beyond and shuddered. Probably mice, or even rats, after the crumbs. She didn't want to know which, she wanted to turn around and run out the door as quickly as her legs would take her.

Instead, she stepped forward and hurried through the empty rooms, determined to find the bag and return home to her hungry baby. She could hear squeaks and groans, the old house seemed to have a life of its own. It certainly wasn't empty, it had plenty of inhabitants. And now that the party was over and the humans had left, they were reclaiming their territory.

Lucy paused at the parlor door and explored the cavernous room with her flashlight, praying she would not encounter any pairs of glowing eyes. All clear. She was about a third of the way through the room when she heard something and instinctively stopped in her tracks, straining her ears.

Nothing. She must have been mistaken. She advanced a few steps, and she heard it again. A crunching noise, like footsteps on gravel. It seemed to be coming from outside.

She pointed the flashlight at the long windows, but the blank glass only bounced the reflection back at her.

Lucy took a few more steps toward the drawing-room door on the opposite wall, and again heard the noise. When she moved, she heard the steps. When she stopped, they stopped. It was almost as if someone on the outside of the house was following her movements inside. She began to shiver and she felt the little hairs on the back of her neck stand up. Lucy could hear herself breathing; her breaths sounded loud, like roars. Her heart was pounding in her chest. She couldn't move, she couldn't even scream.

Then she heard a sound she recognized—Toby's giggle.

"Cut it out!" she yelled, as the adrenaline drained away in a great wave of relief. "Toby, I know it's you out there!"

There was no answer, but after a minute or two she heard the boys running away. Great, she muttered to herself. So much for Barney's promise to keep an eye on the boys. It was getting late and they ought to be home in bed.

Finally reaching the doorway, she paused and cast the light over and under chairs and tables, searching for the pink gingham diaper bag. She found it in the corner, exactly where she had left it, and dashed into the room to retrieve it. She was bending to pick it up when she sensed a presence behind her. She whirled around, fully intending to give the boys a scolding.

"You boys should be ashamed . . ." she began, when there was a sudden explosion of bright, white light.

CHAPTER THIRTY-FIVE

Lucy loved sniffing the clean scent of duplicating fluid, and she loved running her fingers over the slick smoothness of the paper. In a moment, when Mrs. Birchall gave the signal, she would open her eyes, turn over the paper, and begin work on the quiz.

Always a good student, full of curiosity and eager to learn, Lucy enjoyed the challenge posed by tests and quizzes. A bright child, she had soon discovered that even if she didn't know the answer she could usually figure it out, or make a good guess. But what was taking Mrs. Birchall so long? Lucy opened her eyes a crack to take a peek.

Something was wrong. She wasn't in Mrs. Birchall's third-grade classroom. Even with her eyes wide open she couldn't see a thing. It was too dark. And her head throbbed. She probed cautiously with her fingers, and discovered a huge lump on her temple.

She had been dreaming. That explained it. She was flat on her back, in the dark, and she had a wicked headache. What she needed was some aspirin, and a big drink of water. Still groggy, she tried to sit up, but the effort made her head spin. She felt queasy. Her breasts tingled as her milk let down, and she reached for baby Zoe.

There was no baby beside her; Bill wasn't there, either. There was only emptiness. She was lying on something hard, and gritty. She smelled dust, and something else, the reek of duplicating fluid. Panicking, she felt around with her hands. It was a dirt floor, a hard-packed dirt floor. Where was she? Why wasn't she in bed?

Once again she tried to sit up, and this time she succeeded. She was dizzy, but she could manage. She reached out with her arms and her hand met a rough wooden wall. She shifted herself around and leaned against it, trying to push down her fear and sort out her thoughts.

The last thing she remembered was returning to the Hallett House and searching for the diaper bag. Poor Zoe. She must be frantic with hunger by now. She had to get back to her.

Lucy pulled herself to her feet and began feeling her way along the wall. Wherever she was, she had to find a way out. She came to a corner, turned, and then found another. It was hard to judge distances, but she seemed to be in a rather small shed, or maybe a closet. Groping with her fingers, she found the door. She reached for the knob, but found an old-fashioned latch, instead. It lifted, and she pushed against the door, but it didn't open. She was locked in.

She leaned against the door, resting her forehead against it. This whole thing was crazy. Someone had knocked her on the head, and locked her in something that seemed to be Ezekiel Hallett's retreat, the old cabin he had insisted on preserving inside his fancy Victorian mansion.

Was this a joke, a prank of some kind? Certainly the boys would never do anything like this. Lucy pounded on the door with her fist. "Let me out!" she screamed. "Let me out!"

She coughed, choking on dust and fumes. The duplicating fluid. Alcohol. Smoke.

Her heart raced. She began to pound harder on the door. Her head was clear now; she knew she had to get out. Her fear gave her strength, and she beat her fists against the plank door as hard as she could.

"Help! Help!" she yelled, at the top of her lungs. Pounding on the door didn't help, so she kicked at it. Coughing and sputtering, she pulled her shirt up and held it over her mouth. It was getting very smoky. She had to get out. She only had minutes.

Stay low, she remembered. Crouching, she threw her whole body against the door, desperately trying to crash through. She did it again and again. Her shoulder throbbed. She was getting dizzy. She collapsed against the door. There was no air. She had to get out. She had to get back to Zoe, and Bill. She sobbed. One more time. She had to try one more time. She couldn't give up.

She tried to gather her last bit of strength for one more assault on the door, but she couldn't move. It was so hot, and there was no air. Something was pressing on her chest, getting tighter and tighter, and she couldn't get her breath. If she could just get one breath she could try again.

The door shuddered. There was a splintering, ripping noise, and chunks of wood crashed around her.

"Breathe in," barked a male voice, as something was placed over her nose. Sweet, fresh air. She sucked it in.

CHAPTER THIRTY-SIX

A noisy cart, rattling down the hallway woke Lucy around seven o'clock. She knew right away she was in the cottage hopital, where her babies had been born, but couldn't remember how she got there.

Her mouth was dry, and she had a raging sore throat. She spotted the water pitcher on the bedstand, but was unable to reach it. Her left arm was taped tightly to her chest, and her right hand was encumbered with an IV tube. She leaned back against the pillow and took inventory. Her head throbbed and she was sore all over, but her most immediate problem was with her breasts. It had been quite a while since she had last nursed Zoe and they were painfully full.

Poor Zoe must be starving, she thought. She had to get home. She looked for a call button, found it safety-pinned near her pillow and rang for the nurse.

"How are we doing this morning?" inquired the nurse. She was a brisk woman in her early fifties, whose short gray hair was cut in a no-nonsense style.

"Thirsty," croaked Lucy, surprised at the sound of her voice.

"I'll bet you are," said the nurse, as she raised the bed to a sitting position and rolled the tray table closer to Lucy. She poured a glass of water, and held it for Lucy. "Sips, dear, tiny sips."

She let Lucy take five or six sips, and then set the glass on the table. Lucy immediately reached for it, but a deep, racking cough shook her body and filled her mouth with phlegm. The nurse handed her a tissue, and Lucy spat out a wad of gray-tinged mucous.

"Ugh," said Lucy, rather alarmed.

"From the fire," the nurse explained. "You inhaled quite a lot of smoke."

"What happened?" asked Lucy. "I don't remember a fire. Are the kids all right?"

"I don't really know the details," said the nurse. "I only came on duty a few minutes ago. You'll have to talk to the doctor."

"I have a little baby. I need to get home to her," said Lucy.

The nurse shook her head sympathetically. "The doctor will be in soon. Meanwhile, you're supposed to take these." She held out a cup containing two white pills. "For pain."

Lucy obediently took the pills in her mouth and swallowed them down with a swig of water. The nurse patted her hand, and left the room. Lucy closed her eyes and hoped the pills would work soon.

She started to drift off, when a startle reflex shook her body and jerked her awake. Fire. The nurse had said fire. Her stomach felt hollow and she began to breathe rapidly. Where was the fire? Why hadn't they told her? What were they keeping from her? She had to know what happened, and whether Bill and the kids were all right.

She reached for the call button, but fell asleep before she could ring.

When she woke a few hours later Doc Ryder was standing over her. "Up to your old shenanigans," he said, waggling a finger at her. An old-fashioned country GP, Doc Ryder had delivered Lucy's babies, stitched up Toby's foot when he cut it on a broken bottle while swimming at the lake, and prescribed countless bottles of sticky pink antibiotic syrup for ear infections. He flipped open Lucy's chart and reviewed it.

"Looks like you'll live," he said. "But you're going to feel pretty miserable for a couple of days. You've got a concussion there, and a dislocated shoulder. We've got that strapped up, should heal nicely. Smoke inhalation's tricky, though. Don't want you to get pneumonia, got you on antibiotics through the IV."

"Can I go home?" asked Lucy.

"We're just going to take things one day at a time," he said. "I want to keep an eye on that concussion. Give you a chance to rest."

"The baby needs me," said Lucy.

"Now, now," he said, patting her hand. "Why don't you let us take care of you for a change?"

She wanted to tell him that a nursing mother and baby needed to be together, bound as they were by the law of supply and demand, but she couldn't summon the energy to argue before he was gone. All alone, she tried to remember what had brought her to the hospital. The nurse said she had been in a fire, but she couldn't remember when or where. And why was Doc Ryder so evasive when she asked if she could go home? Did she still have a home, or had it burned down? And why couldn't she have the baby? Was Zoe all right?

Spotting the telephone on the bedstand, she pulled herself up until she could reach it. Her first attempt to punch in the number failed, and she blinked back tears of frustration. Taking a deep breath she tried again, but only got a busy signal. Relieved, she dropped back onto the pillows. Everything must be okay if somebody was talking on the phone, she decided. Reassured, she closed her eyes to go back to sleep. She was so tired. Between sleep and consciousness she heard the insistent beep of the busy signal. She saw the wall phone at home; the receiver was dangling.

She started, suddenly wide awake. The busy signal didn't mean anything, she realized. All it meant was that the receiver was off the hook. For all she knew, the house could have burned down around it. She remembered Lenk sneering at her. "This is all your fault," he'd said. "You and that husband of yours." She wanted to try calling again, but didn't have the energy to reach for the awkwardly placed phone. She felt tears pricking her eyes and lifted her hands to brush them away, but her hand dropped to her chest as she fell asleep.

Waking a few hours later, Lucy once again assessed her condition. Her headache had subsided; it was still there but it was manageable. The same with her throat. It only hurt when she swallowed. Breathing was a bit of a problem; her breathing passages were raw and she was painfully aware of each breath. Her breasts were tender and a constant reminder of how much she missed her baby.

"So, how's Sleeping Beauty?" inquired the gray-haired nurse with a warm smile.

"Better," she said with a wan smile. "Could you hand me the phone?"

"First things first," said the nurse, producing a thermometer. "Open wide."

Conversation was temporarily shut off as the nurse tended to Lucy's needs. Finally, she tucked the sheet around her and pulled out the thermometer.

"Hmm," she said, making a notation on Lucy's chart.

"What does that mean?" asked Lucy.

"Looking good," said the nurse, with a grin. "I'd tell you if I could, but it's against hospital policy. Only the doctor can discuss your condition with you."

"Can you tell me anything about last night? About why I'm here? I'm so afraid something has happened to my family."

The nurse shook her head sympathetically. "I don't know, but I'll see what I can find out. Meanwhile, why don't you call?" She placed the phone on the bed, next to Lucy.

"Thanks," Lucy said. She punched in the familiar numbers, but all she got was the same busy signal. She tried Sue's number, but there was no answer. In desperation she dialed her mother's number, long distance to New York, thinking she would have heard if there was a tragedy. She let the phone ring and ring, she counted thirty times, and then gave up.

She was sitting, staring at the phone in her lap, when the door opened. An orderly brought in a lunch tray, set it on the table in front of her, and lifted the cover.

Lucy leaned forward; she was hungry and eager to see what was for lunch. There was milk, in a little carton, and a plastic cup of tea. Also a small container of orange juice and two slices of white bread in plastic wrap with a pat of margarine on top. The entree appeared to be a slice of meatlike substance smothered in thick pinkinsh-tan gravy, surrounded by rounded humps of red cabbage, instant mashed potatoes, and a tiny bowl of stewed tomatoes. Dessert was a bowl of applesauce.

Lucy took a sip of tea and a spoonful of applesauce. It was unsweetened. She looked for sugar, but there wasn't any. She poked at the mystery meat with her fork but the thought of eating it made her nauseous. She pushed the tray away and sank back onto the pillow.

She punched out her number on the phone and again got the busy signal. She couldn't stand it; she had to know what had happened. She felt incomplete without her family, especially the baby. Her little round head, her fuzzy hair, her fat baby cheeks. They had rarely been apart—Lucy was used to nursing whenever and wherever Zoe seemed hungry. They were rarely apart—Zoe spent a good part of the day in the baby-carrier, nestled under Lucy's chin.

She felt much stronger, she decided, wiggling her toes. There didn't seem to be anything the matter with her legs. She bent her knees, and stretched her legs out. The movement hurt. She flexed her ankles, and walked her feet up and down the bed, trying to work out the soreness.

She eyed the IV tube in her hand. The needle, she saw, was held in place by a big piece of tape. She raised her hand to her mouth and took hold of a corner of tape with her teeth. She gave a little tug and it pulled away. In a matter of seconds she had peeled the tape off.

She looked at the needle sticking into her hand. Carefully, she bit down on the plastic collar that connected the needle to the tubing and gave her head a quick jerk. The needle came out smoothly. Lucy watched a bead of blood well up, and licked it away. No more blood appeared.

She swung her legs over the side of the bed and stood up, feeling an immediate draft on her bare backside. So far, so good. She wasn't even dizzy. She opened the bedside stand and found a plastic bag containing her clothes.

Opening it, she grimaced. The baseball shirt and pants. What had she been dressed for? A costume party? She wrinkled her nose. They stank of smoke. Too bad, they would have to do.

Getting dressed with only one arm was a bit tricky, she discovered. Leaning her fanny against the bed she pulled on the tight pants, first tugging one leg and then the other. Socks didn't seem worth the trouble; she jammed her bare feet into her sneakers. The bra would be impossible so she ignored it and pulled the striped shirt over her head, leaving the left arm empty. She sat for a minute on the chair, holding her purse in her lap. Then, taking a deep breath she stood up and headed for the door.

Hearing voices approaching, she froze in her tracks. Thinking quickly she climbed back in bed and pulled the covers up over her. The johnny was on the floor but it was too late to do anything about it. The door was opening.

"Oh, didn't I put this in the laundry?" asked the nurse, picking it up. She shook her head. "Sometimes I think I'd forget my head if it wasn't fastened on! I forgot your meds—here you go."

She held out the little white cup with two pills and Lucy tossed them back, following with a swallow of water from a second cup.

"I'm so sorry," said the nurse. "I hope you weren't too uncomfortable."

Lucy shook her head. "I'm feeling much better."

"Not much appetite, I see," she said, indicating the tray.

"I just can't," Lucy said apologetically.

"Never mind. I'll take this away and let you get some rest." She picked up the tray and swept out of the room.

Lucy waited for a few minutes after the nurse left, then got up very cautiously. She tiptoed to the door and peeked out. The hall was empty, blocked by double doors at either end. A clutter of wheelchairs and a meds cart at one end seemed to indicate the nurses' station, so she went the other way.

Pushing through the doors she found a staircase. She went down a floor, backtracked through another hallway, and found herself in the lobby. She sat down in an armchair and considered her next step.

Call a taxi? She checked her wallet. Two bucks. No problem, they probably took VISA. She spotted a pay phone and stood up. The room whirled around her. Maybe she wasn't in such good shape after all. She waited a minute or two and the dizziness subsided. Careful not to move too fast she made her way to the phone. The number for the taxi company was conveniently printed on a sign above the phone. She was rummaging for a dime when she heard a voice.

"Lucy! What are you doing here?" It was Doug Durning.

"I don't really know," said Lucy. "They said I was in a fire."

"Really? The Hallett House burned down last night. Were you there?"

"I guess I must have been," said Lucy, as memories of the party flooded back. She looked down at the baseball outfit. "I wore this as a costume."

"That was some costume Bill wore—a giant bumblebee. He's got some balls, that's all I can say."

"Was anybody hurt in the fire—besides me, I mean?" Lucy grabbed his hand. "Is my family okay?"

"Sure," Doug said. "Why wouldn't they be?"

"I don't know," Lucy admitted. She couldn't help smiling foolishly; she felt light-headed with relief. "They wouldn't tell me anything here. I got a little crazy, I guess. I just want to go home."

"Can I give you a lift?" Doug's brow was furrowed with concern. "You look a bit shaky to be out on your own."

"I feel a bit shaky," confessed Lucy, gratefully taking his arm. "This is really nice of you."

"No problem," said Doug, carefully supporting her as he led her out to his car.

CHAPTER THIRTY-SEVEN

Seated in Doug's aging Saab, Lucy felt unaccountably weepy. Embarrassed, she brushed away her tears.

"I'm sorry," she said. "I'm an awful mess."

"It's probably the medication," said Doug, starting the engine.

That was probably it, thought Lucy, wondering what they had been pumping into her. Whatever it was, it was taking her on an emotional roller-coaster ride. "Thanks for the lift," she said. "I can't tell you how much I appreciate it."

"It's nothing," said Doug, turning smoothly out of the parking lot. "So, what happened to you?"

"I don't know. I really can't remember much. They said I was in a fire."

"Like I said, the Hallett House burned down last night. It was a total loss."

"Oh." Lucy sat stunned. Poor Monica had died in a fire . . . the same thing could have happened to her.

"A bunch of kids discovered it. They called the fire department. Probably saved your life."

"I was lucky," said Lucy, wondering what she had been doing at the mansion. She should have been home.

"Yeah," said Doug. "Say, why don't we take a look at the place? Survey the damage. It's right off this road."

"I don't want to go there," said Lucy, as her stomach gave a lurch. "Could you take me home first? It's just a little bit farther."

Doug's hand tightened on the steering wheel. "This'll only take a minute," he said, making a sharp turn. They bounced along the rough dirt road and pulled up in front of the blackened pile of rubble that had once been the magnificent Hallett House, the finest house in Tinker's Cove.

"Oh, my God," gasped Lucy, shocked at the sight. "I can't believe I survived that."

Absolutely nothing was left, even the chimneys had cracked from the intense heat and collapsed. It was all gone—the fanciful pillared tower, the widow's walk, the ornate portico. Everything was reduced to soot and cinders, surrounded by a thin ribbon of yellow tape.

"It was quite a fire," said Doug. There was an odd note of satisfaction in his tone. "You should have seen it," he said, nodding. "Flames forty, fifty feet high. It was something." He gestured excitedly with his arms, and Lucy caught a whiff of something pungent. What was it? she wondered. It was so familiar.

A small group of bystanders had gathered. They stood, exchanging only brief bits of conversation, occasionally shaking their heads.

"They had to call in fire companies from Wilton and Gilead and even Rockland," said Doug. "But even with all that extra help they couldn't save it."

"You sound almost pleased," said Lucy.

Doug jerked abruptly and looked sharply at her; she wondered if she'd said something wrong.

He shrugged. "The town's better off without it. It was an eyesore." He started the engine.

"I guess," said Lucy, yawning. She was very tired. She was having trouble keeping her eyes open. She leaned back and closed them, just for a minute. She felt the car begin to move. Soon she would be home.

A jumble of images crowded her mind. She could hear Zoe crying, but she couldn't find her. She was stumbling through a maze of rooms that opened before her, tilted at crazy angles like a carnival fun house. She was running uphill, then downhill and someone was pursuing her, laughing. It was Mrs. Birchall, her third-grade teacher. There was a horrible, choking smell. Mimeo fluid. She opened her eyes.

She was still in the car, but she was lying across the front seat. Through the window she saw dark green—balsam and fir trees—and blue sky. They were parked somewhere in the woods.

She felt a rush of cold air as the car door opened. She tilted her head to look behind her. She saw Doug. His face was red and angry. He was holding a length of two by four. "Nosey bitch," he said, raising his arm.

Instinctively, Lucy rolled away as Doug slammed the wood down on the seat where her head had been. Grabbing the dashboard with her good arm she pulled herself upright. Turning, she spotted Doug outside the car and watched him warily, waiting for his next move.

To her surprise, he dropped the two by four and fumbled in his pocket. Pulling out a book of matches he carefully and deliberately tore one off and struck it, then tossed it in the car. Lucy followed it with her gaze and saw it land in the back seat, which, she discovered, he had loaded with firewood and scrap lumber. The reek of mimeo fluid filled the air.

As she watched, the orange flame of the match grew larger. It turned blue, spreading along a piece of scrap wood, then leaped onto a branch of dry tinder that caught immediately with a snapping sound. A whitish gray column of smoke formed and began filling the car. Durning slammed the door and stepped back. His eyes were wide open, his expression eager with anticipation. He licked his lips.

Lucy reached for the door handle on the passenger side but couldn't find it. Blinking, her eyes already smarting, she discovered it was broken. Through the smoke she saw Durning laughing. Coughing, she grabbed the steering wheel and pulled herself toward the driver's side door. The horn blared. Awkwardly, she fumbled for the lock with her right hand. The back seat was now fully ablaze, the car was like a furnace. The smoke was so thick that she could no longer see. Groping with her fingers, she found the latch. She pushed against the door and the lock finally yielded; she fell out of the car onto her knees.

Retching and choking, still blinded by the smoke, she tried to crawl away from the heat of the fire. Durning stopped her, grabbing her by the hair and pulling her to her feet.

"What's your hurry?" he asked. "Don't you like the pretty fire?"

"Let me go!" she screamed. "You're crazy! You're going to get us both killed!"

"Not both of us," he said, shoving her back toward the car and raising his arm to hit her. Staggering, she threw up her good arm to block the blow, but it never came. Instead, she saw Bill materialize in the smoke and grab Durning by the shoulders, throwing him back against a tree. He hit him twice in the stomach, and then punched him in the face. Durning's head snapped back and he slid to the ground. Bill stood over him, fists clenched, breathing hard. His eyes were narrow slits, and his jaw was clenched. Lucy could see a vein in his neck pulsing.

A sudden roar made her turn her head, and she saw the Saab disappear in a rush of bright orange flames. Black smoke filled the air. Bill grabbed her arm and dragged her away from the burning car.

"Oh my God," she said, feeling her knees start to buckle underneath her. He caught her in his arms. Lucy leaned against him, drinking in his strong, sweaty smell. She nuzzled her face against his beard, and felt the smooth flannel covering his chest under her fingertips. He tightened his arms around her.

"I want to go home," whispered Lucy.

CHAPTER THIRTY-EIGHT

Being home was bliss, thought Lucy later that afternoon as she looked down at Zoe's sweet little head. She was sitting sideways on the couch, with her legs stretched out. Zoe was propped on pillows, because of Lucy's taped arm, and was enthusiastically making up for missed meals. Edna, Bill's mother, hovered nearby, ready to assist.

"Would you like some more juice?" she asked. "How about some lemonade?"

"That would be great," said Lucy. She had an enormous thirst; she couldn't drink enough.

Edna bustled off, pleased to have an errand.

"I told Bill," she said, when she returned. "I told him the hospital wouldn't know what to do with you. Bring her home, I said, so she can be with the baby. If Lucy takes care of the baby, we can take care of Lucy. That's what I said."

"All I could think of was getting back home," said Lucy, after she'd gulped down half the lemonade. "I felt like one of those trapped foxes that chews off its leg to get back to her babies."

"It's mother love, dear."

"It's instict," said Toby. "Learned about it in school."

"It's probably a little bit of both," said Lucy, reaching for Toby's hand. "Is everything okay? You look worried."

"You're gonna be okay, aren't you, Mom?"

"Sure," said Lucy.

Toby shifted nervously from one foot to the other. "Are me and the guys in trouble?" he asked.

"What do you mean?" asked Lucy. "Sit down and tell me about it." She patted the side of the couch.

"Are they gonna think we started the fire?" he asked, perching next to her.

"Why would they think that?" A horrible thought flitted through her mind. "You didn't, did you?"

"No. We wouldn't do anything like that. But last year, remember the toilet paper? Everybody thought me and Eddie put it on Mr. Reid's hedge, but it wasn't us. It was really Tim Rogers. He said we'd be real sorry if we told."

"This is different," said Lucy, covering his hand with her own. "This isn't kid stuff."

"I was scared," confessed Toby. "Really scared."

"Me, too," said Lucy. Now that she remembered what had happened last night she didn't want to think about it. She pushed the dark thoughts away, and smiled at Toby. "You boys really gave me a fright."

"Yeah, that was funny. You jumped a mile. You yelled at us and we ran behind some bushes. We heard some footsteps and we thought it was Officer Barney, coming to take us home. We were gonna make him look for us, and then jump out and scare him. But it wasn't Barney—it was some guy. He started carrying cans into the house and we figured he was the one setting the fires. Stubby called the fire department on his walkie-talkie."

"He knew what to do?"

"Sure. Officer Barney lent him a real police radio for his costume. Showed him how to use it and everything."

"I'm surprised the dispatcher believed you—didn't he think it might be a Halloween prank?"

"Yeah." Toby nodded. "He took our names and said we'd be in serious trouble if it was a false alarm. That scared us a little bit, because we waited and waited and nothing seemed to happen. Then the guy ran out and drove away, and still nothing happened. Richie and Eddie said maybe we ought to go home and tell our parents, but I didn't want to leave you there. Then it started to smell like the charcoal fire when Dad lights it, you know there's a fire in there but you can't see much. That's when I really got scared. I wanted to go in and get you, but the guys wouldn't let me. We looked through the window and there were blue and orange flames racing around, up and down the walls and across the floor. They'd start up and go out. It was weird.

"That's when the fire truck came. They made us stand back and we saw them go in with oxygen tanks on their backs. They went in and then the whole place seemed to explode. There was a big whoosh, and all at once it was really on fire. That's when the fireman carried you out. I saw him in the doorway, with the red flames behind him."

"Wow," said Lucy, reaching up and pulling his head down for a quick kiss. "You boys did the right thing. You were really brave."

"I'm just glad you're okay. You really are okay, aren't you?"

"Yeah," said Lucy. "I'm gonna be fine."

"That's good," said Toby, " 'cause Mom, you don't look too good right now."

"I don't feel too good, either," admitted Lucy. "I wonder where your dad is with those prescriptions."

Lucy ached all over, her throat was raw and she was uncomfortably aware of her chest as she breathed. Her shoulder throbbed, and her head was pounding.

"You look bushed, Lucy. Let me take the baby and put her down in the crib," offered Edna. "She's sleeping like an angel."

Toby wandered off, and Edna carried the baby upstairs, leaving Lucy alone. She glanced around the room—it was getting a bit shabby. The couch was worn, the rug needed a cleaning, the pictures were just a bit askew. Magazines were piled in an untidy heap on the lamp table, a pair of Elizabeth's shoes lay forgotten under the coffee table. It had never looked better.

"So, how ya doin'?" asked Bill, appearing in the doorway.

"Fine. It's great to be home. Baby's sleeping."

"About time," said Bill, sitting down heavily in the recliner, still holding a plastic shopping bag.

"Did you get everything?"

"Yup." He began unpacking. "Antibiotics, pain killer, ice bag, heating pad, disposable diapers. You know, I couldn't find a single diaper anywhere in the house!"

"I know—that's why I went to the Hallett House. I left the diaper bag there."

"I knew there had to be a reason. I thought you might have gone after Toby. That was some night." He shook his head. "Phone call woke me up, I didn't know what was going on. Girls were frantic, baby was soaking wet and screaming, cops brought Toby home, you were at the hospital. It was crazy."

Lucy nodded. She was content to look at Bill. Always the same outfit—jeans, plaid flannel shirt, work boots, beard. Except in summer. Then it was shorts, T-shirt, work boots, and beard. He never changed. He was steady and reliable. Strong. Always gentle with her and the kids. In all the years they'd been married she'd never seen him strike anyone, until today.

"I didn't know you could fight," said Lucy.

"Neither did I. Pure adrenaline." Bill's cheeks reddened and he fingered a brown plastic medicine vial. "I didn't want to stop hitting him. I coulda killed him."

"How did you find me?"

"Mom sent me to the hospital to bring you home. I saw you getting in the car with him. I called your name, but I was too far away and you didn't hear me. I decided to follow. I couldn't figure out what was going on. Why did you leave with him?"

"Nobody would tell me anything and I was going crazy—I thought they were keeping something from me. I was afraid Lenk had burned the house down and I was the only one left. I had to get home and find out what had happened."

"Why didn't you call?"

"I tried and tried but all I got was a busy signal."

"Oh." Bill blushed. "I was on the phone for quite a while trying to get things organized, and as soon as I got off the phone the kids took over."

"I should have thought of that," said Lucy.

"Anyway, I pulled into the parking lot and saw you getting into Doug's car. I figured he was just bringing you home, but I didn't feel good about you being in the car with him. I don't know why—I just felt uneasy. I started thinking as I was following you and it was pretty clear that he had the most to gain from the fires."

"He did?"

"Sure. Because of the bylaws. Getting rid of his house gave him a clean slate. He could pretty much build what he wanted, long as it was white and had shutters."

"The Red Zone!" exclaimed Lucy. "I can't believe I was so dumb."

"I don't get it."

"It was on the movie marquee. The Red Zone. I looked right at it."

"Zoning by fire," said Bill thoughtfully. "That's what he was doing. Come to think of it, I heard something about him buying the Hallett House."

"I heard him talking to Krissy at the party—all about how the property was worth more without the building!"

"That's right. Burning it down gave him a very nice piece of commercial property. It was a pretty clever plan—everybody thought there was a pyromaniac loose. Then Lenk started spouting off and everybody thought it was him."

"I think it started out as a rational plan," Lucy said, "but it got out of control. He liked setting those fires. I'll never forget the expression on his face when he started the fire in the car. It was creepy."

"I think he had some idea of killing you at the Hallett House but there were too many people so he headed off down that old dirt track into the woods. That was scary. I couldn't get too close or he'd see me but I was terrified of losing him. I called the cops on the phone in the truck and decided to follow on foot. Then I saw the smoke and panicked—I was afraid I was too late. When I saw him trying to hit you it was like a movie or something. I didn't even realize what I was doing."

"You were great," said Lucy.

"I wouldn't want to make a career of it," said Bill, flexing his hands and massaging his knuckles. "Thank God for cell phones—

I was real happy when the cops came and took him off my hands." He reached for the remote control and pushed the chair back so the leg rest came up. He flipped through the channels until he found the NFL game.

In her nest of pillows and blankets on the couch, Lucy snuggled down and closed her eyes. She started to drift off, then jerked awake. She blinked. She was home. She could hear the girls' arguing upstairs. Edna was running the mixer in the kitchen. Bill was snoring in the chair, a shaving cream commercial was playing on the TV. Everything was fine.

EPILOGUE

Outside, a fine dusting of snow, the first of the season, was softly falling.

Inside Miss Tilley's house a fire was burning brightly, the tea was hot, and the scones were dripping with butter. Lucy reached for another, and Sue's eyebrows shot up in disapproval.

"I can't help it," said Lucy. "I'm hungry all the time. I think it's from working out. I haven't lost any weight, but I feel great."

"Isn't it about time to wean that child?" asked Miss Tilley. "Franklin Delano Roosevelt's mother nursed him until he was two, you know. Look how he turned out." Miss Tilley had regained much of her snap and vigor, and about ten pounds, since she had arranged for Rachel Goodman to come in for a couple of hours every day.

"You mean how he became President of the United States?" asked Rachel, her eyes sparkling mischievously.

"Rode into office on Teddy's coattails," said Miss Tilley, with a wave of her hand. "He was always a momma's boy, and he packed the Supreme Court with Communists and tried to destroy the free enterprise system." She took a healthy bite of scone and chewed happily; once again the Republicans were in charge and the nation was back on course. "And that wife of his," she paused and rolled her eyes. "Eleanor!"

"My grandfather didn't think much of her, either," admitted Lucy. "He used to say Eleanor Roosevelt and John Dewey practically ruined the country."

"Sound man," said Miss Tilley, nodding. "Is he . . . ?"

"No." Lucy shook her head. "He's been dead for quite a while, but he always used to say that he liked Ike."

"We all did," said Miss Tilley, smiling at the memory of the Supreme Allied Commander turned politician.

"So, Lucy, how are you feeling?" asked Rachel, bringing in a fresh pot of tea.

"Fine. Krissy and Vicki gave me some special exercises. I'm sure I recovered faster because of them. My shoulder's a little stiff, but that's all."

"You were lucky," said Rachel. "I didn't want the boys to stay out after the party, but it was a good thing they did. Imagine what could have happened if they hadn't been there. . . ."

"I know," said Lucy. "It's still hard for me to believe it all wasn't a really bad dream. A nightmare. He tried to kill me twice. I never suspected him for a minute. I thought he was a nice guy. I was grateful when he offered to give me a ride home from the hospital."

"You kept telling me it was poor Dr. Mayes," said Sue.

"Well, I did suspect him at first, especially when I learned about Krissy," admitted Lucy. "I think even his daughter, Mira, had her suspicions. I'm glad it wasn't him. And then I was sure it was

Randy Lenk, and the police thought so, too. He was making those anonymous phone calls and his father died in a fire and he lives in that weird house full of junk. But when I opened my eyes and saw Doug holding that two by four over my head, well, that convinced me he was the arsonist. Plus, the fact that he'd filled the car with firewood and soaked it with mimeo fluid was also a clue."

"He was going to burn you up?" Rachel's dark eyes were huge.

"In the car, after he'd bashed my head in." Lucy shuddered. "He was trying to make it look like an accident."

"A very wicked man," said Miss Tilley. "Now that I think of it he was a sneaky little boy. I used to find him in the adult book section, sneaking peeks at *Peyton Place*."

"You allowed a book like that in the library?" Lucy was surprised.

"I did. Of course, nobody had the nerve to take it out."

The women laughed.

"And how is Jennifer? She always reminded me a little bit of Alison in the book," said Miss Tilley.

"So you read *Peyton Place*?" Lucy pounced on her.

"Of course. I used to read all the books that I bought for the library before putting them out on the shelves."

"Jennifer's home," said Rachel, who lived across the street from the Mitchells. "She's one brave little girl. She's got pins in her legs—it looks dreadful—but she's absolutely confident that she'll walk again. I saw her playing field hockey in the garage in her wheelchair with a bunch of her friends the other day."

"That was a terrible accident," said Lucy, who immediately wished she could take the words back. Miss Tilley had fallen silent, and was staring at the window.

"Just look at that snow," said Sue, changing the subject. "Isn't it pretty? Soon it will be Christmas!" She loved all holidays, but especially Christmas when she decorated her house lavishly and set up three Christmas trees.

"What will happen to Doug?" asked Rachel.

"They have to decide if he's crazy," said Lucy. "He's been sent to the state hospital for psychiatric tests."

"I don't think an insanity defense will play very well," said Sue, tapping a scarlet nail against Miss Tilley's blue Canton china cup. "He had a solid financial motive, and the fires were all carefully planned."

"That's right," agreed Miss Tilley. "He was determined to develop that property. When the commission said no, he decided to take matters into his own hands and burn it down. Such a shame."

"I don't understand," said Rachel.

"Neither did I," said Lucy. "Until Bill explained the bylaw to me. As long as Durning's antique house was standing, the commission would only let him make changes that were appropriate to the period it was built. But once the house was gone, he had a valuable piece of commercially zoned property right in the center of town. He could build pretty much whatever he wanted, as long as he followed the commission's style guidelines."

"That's right," said Miss Tilley. "That house was a fine old Captain's home built in 1830. He wanted to remodel it into an office complex. It was quite ambitious. There was even a bank, with an ATM machine and a drive-through window. There was going to be a big parking lot—the entire character of the house would have been destroyed."

"So you turned him down?" asked Rachel.

"Of course. We had no choice. But the bylaw did create a dangerous situation, although we didn't realize it at the time. If a historic building was destroyed—by fire or hurricane or Act of God—and couldn't be repaired, then the owner would have a lot more leeway. The commission standards for new construction aren't nearly as strict."

"The ATM would have been okay?" Sue asked.

"As long as it was painted white and had shutters," said Lucy, echoing Bill.

"That's right," agreed Miss Tilley.

"But why all the other fires?" asked Rachel. "He burned down half the town."

"Camouflage," said Sue, with a knowing nod.

"Barney said they're investigating to see if he had financial interests in some of the other buildings. The Hallett House was owned by a realty trust—it's complicated but they suspect Durning would have profited from that fire, too."

"One person who hasn't made out very well is Randy Lenk," said Rachel. "I met Ted at the bank and he said state inspectors found gasoline leaking from his underground tanks. He's going to have to pay for a very expensive cleanup."

"Don't bet on it," said Sue derisively. "When I stopped in for gas the other day, he tried to sell me the station. At a bargain price. Nice of him, don't you think?"

"Not very . . . you would have got stuck with the cleanup," said Lucy.

"That's the plan. I bet he'll find some poor sucker who thinks he's getting a deal. Lenk wants to move to Idaho or someplace. Said he's sick and tired of the government poking into everything, and there's some other folks out there that think like him. They're forming some militia or something, they're going to reclaim the government for the people, he said."

"Well, they better make him general," said Miss Tilley. "He can't abide taking directions from anyone. Never could."

The women fell silent, and Rachel got up to put a fresh log on the fire.

"I bet you haven't heard," said Sue. "The selectmen have appointed me to the Recreation Commission."

"Congratulations," said Lucy. "That's the perfect job for you."

"I think so," Sue agreed. "In fact, I'm already making plans for a big town picnic in the spring. Lucy's prime suspect, Dr. Mayes, has donated the Homestead property to the town, for a conservation area. Isn't that neat?"

"That's a wonderful way to remember Monica," said Lucy.

"I think so. We're going to put up a nice sign, you'll have to help us with the wording, okay, Lucy?"

"Sure."

"And maybe you could make some cupcakes for the picnic? Say, six dozen?"

Lucy met Sue's eyes, and she smiled. "I'll donate soda, paper plates, napkins, whatever you need. I'll even bake brownies, but cupcakes?" She gave her head a little shake. "Never again."

Please see the next page for
an exciting sneak preview
of Leslie Meier's newest
Lucy Stone mystery
BACK TO SCHOOL MURDER
on sale October 1997
wherever hardcover mysteries are sold!

CHAPTER ONE

"Unexpectedly, at home," typed Lucy Stone. "Chester Neal, aged 85 years." She paused and brushed away an annoying strand of hair. It was stifling in the newspaper office and it wasn't even nine o'clock.

"Ted? I'm not sure about this wording. Shouldn't we put 'suddenly' instead of 'unexpectedly'? How can death be unexpected when you're eighty-five?"

"I'd say it was pretty unexpected for Chet," replied Ted Stillings, the fortyish publisher, editor, and chief reporter for *The Pennysaver*.

"Really? How did he die?" asked Lucy, leaning back and fanning herself with the press release from McCoul's Funeral Home.

"Fell off a ladder."

"A ladder? What was he doing on a ladder at his age?"

"Picking apples, of course."

"Oh."

"And from what I hear, the family's pretty upset. Especially his father."

"His father!" exclaimed Lucy.

"Just kidding," said Ted, patting his pockets. "Camera bag, beeper, pens, notebook . . . I think I've got everything. I'll be over at district court, covering the arraignments. The morning after Labor Day is always pretty busy. If something comes up, call my beeper number, okay?"

"Okay," said Lucy, turning back to the obituaries. Poor Chet would be missed by a lot of people in the little seaside village of Tinker's Cove, Maine. He belonged to the Masons, the Chamber of Commerce, the Men's Forum, and the Village Improvement Society. He was also a deacon at the Community Church and a trustee of the Broadbrooks Free Library.

"Hi, Lucy! Isn't this weather awful?"

Lucy looked up from the computer and welcomed Karen Baker with a broad smile. Karen's face was pink with the heat, and her blond pageboy hung limply.

"Hi, Karen. Never fails. As soon as summer is officially over and the kids go back to school, we get a heat wave."

"You know, I think you're right. What are you doing here? I didn't know you were working at the paper."

"It's just for a few days. Ted asked me to fill in for Phyllis. Her mother's sick. What can I do for you?"

"I've got an announcement for the PTA Bake Sale this weekend. Am I too late for this week's paper?"

"Not a bit," said Lucy, quickly checking the scribbled announcement for date, time, and place.

"What have you done with little Miss Zoë?" asked Karen. Her daughter, Jennifer, and Lucy's next-to-youngest daughter,

Sara, were best friends. Zoë, Lucy's two-year-old, was a favorite with both Jenn and her mother.

"She's at the new day-care center, over at the Rec Building. It's pretty nice."

"That's what I hear," said Karen.

"Actually, I'm wracked with guilt," said Lucy, casually propping her chin on her hand.

"They'll take good care of her. Sue Finch is in charge, isn't she?"

"It's not that. I'm suffering guilt pangs because I don't mind leaving my baby. Not one bit. I love it here. Isn't it great? I feel as if I ought to be wearing a little hat like Rosalind Russell in *His Girl Friday.*"

"I never noticed it before, but you're right. This place sure has plenty of atmosphere," said Karen.

Lucy followed her gaze as she took in the dusty venetian blinds that hung from the plate glass window, and the framed front pages commemorating VICTORY IN EUROPE, JAPAN SURRENDERS, and the famous Niskayuna Mills fire that hung on the walls. The space behind the counter was divided into two areas: Ted's with its ancient oak roll-top desk and swivel chair, and Phyllis's, temporarily Lucy's, with an ugly battleship gray steel desk topped with a computer. A police scanner sat on the counter, occasionally emitting hisses and cackles.

"Notice that smell?" asked Lucy. "That's hot lead. From the old linotype machine. Ted says you only smell it in hot weather. But the best part is the bathroom. I get it all to myself—nobody follows me in." At two, Zoë liked to follow her mother everywhere.

Karen chuckled sympathetically. "I know what you mean. It's been a long summer, hasn't it? Seemed like the kids would never go back to school. I had to restrain myself when that beautiful big yellow bus pulled up this morning . . . I was tempted to kiss Moe!"

Lucy grimaced. Moe was a very ugly, very fat school bus driver. "So, how are you going to fill your idle hours, now that the kids are back in school?"

"Well, this morning I took a long shower, and then I had a second cup of coffee and read the newspaper. But I can't really afford to continue this fabulously luxurious lifestyle. I've got to give Country Cousins a call." Like a lot of women in Tinker's Cove, Karen worked part-time for the giant catalog retailer, Country Cousins. "What about you? Are you coming back this year?"

"Probably." Lucy sighed. "'Thank you for calling Country Cousins. My name is Lucy. How may I help you today?'" she recited. "You know what I'd really like? A job that's not just a job. Something interesting and challenging, you know?"

"Sure. Why do you think I've stuck with the PTA all these years? There, I'm somebody. I'm Madam President. Not just 'Karen-what-would-you-like-from-our-catalog.'" She shrugged and tucked a strand of damp hair behind her ear. "Good jobs are hard to find around here."

"I know," agreed Lucy, pausing a moment to listen to the scanner. Just a routine traffic stop. "If I went back to school, I could teach English. I only need a few credits, you know."

"That's a good idea, Lucy. Quite a few of the old fossils at the high school are coming up for retirement."

"Really?"

"Yeah. And you could substitute in the meantime. It's decent pay, and no commitment. If the kids are sick or something, you don't have to go in . School schedule, too. You only work when the kids are in school."

"Maybe I will sign up for that course."

"Which one?"

"Over at Winchester. Tuesday and Thursday nights. 'Victorian Writers (1837–1901), with a special focus on Elizabeth Barrett Browning and Robert Browning.' I saw it when I typeset the ad. I was so tempted—I majored in English lit, you know. But it seemed awfully expensive."

"Education is a good investment," said Karen. "Especially if you could eventually teach. They start at over twenty thousand, plus benefits and summers off. Why, that new assistant principal at the elementary school—Carol Crane—I bet she's barely thirty and she's making forty-two thousand."

"You're kidding." Lucy turned to listen to the scanner. Her attention had been caught by a change in the dispatcher's tone. Usually flat, reciting routine phrases and codes, it had suddenly become imperative.

"Seventeen and Nineteen, report to One-One immediately. Do you copy?"

"What's One-One?" asked Karen.

"Let me see," said Lucy, reaching for a laminated sheet tacked above her desk. She scanned the list and raised an eyebrow. "The elementary school."

"All available units, report to One-One stat, do you copy?"

The two women's eyes locked as they listened to a chorus of voices responding with the single word, "Copy."

"Uh, base, this is Seventeen."

"Seventeen's the chief," explained Lucy.

"Copy, Seventeen. Go ahead."

"Uh, we need fire and rescue over here."

The two women simultaneously took a quick breath.

"Copy. Will relay that message."

"Uh, base?"

"Copy, Seventeen."

"Call the state police for assistance—uh—just get the bomb squad out here real fast! Copy?"

"A bomb at the elementary school?" Karen was incredulous.

"That's what it sounded like," said Lucy, a catch in her throat.

"Jenn's there. And Sara. I'm going over there," announced Karen, hurrying out the door.

"Damn. I'll be along in a minute. I have to call Ted."

Lucy scrabbled frantically among the mess of papers on her desk for the Post-it with Ted's beeper number. She finally found it and punched in the digits. Then she waited, hand on the receiver, for Ted to call back. Her fingers tapped nervously as the minutes ticked by. Sirens filled the air and emergency vehicles screamed down Main Street, blurs of red and yellow as they raced past the office. It was all she could do to wait. She wanted to get to the school, to make sure Sara was all right. Finally, after what seemed like an eternity but was only two minutes, the phone rang.

"Ted! It's about time you called—there's a bomb at the elementary school!"